Praise for Lena Matthews' *Three Nights*

Recommended Read "With *Jokers Wild: Three Nights*, Lena Matthews has written a great book that stands extremely well all on its own, but is even better if you read the first in the series. She has again captured a wonderful sense of a couple falling in love.... The sex scenes are flaming hot, and watching Chris fall victim to the young girl's charms is both realistic and charming."

~ *Leyna, Fallen Angel Reviews*

Four Hearts "Very enjoyable are the stories from this writer (she writes with such a sense of humor) and I recommend this emotional, but satisfying, read."

~ *Glenda K. Bauerle, The Romance Studio*

Five Roses "Lena Matthews' Jokers Wild: Three Nights is a wonderfully fast paced read... Ms. Matthews' depiction of Chris falling victim to the young girl's charms is nothing less than delightful and genuine. I truly enjoyed reading Chris and Eliza's tale..."

~ *Noemi, A Romance Review*

Three Nights
Joker's Wild

Lena Matthews

A SAMHAIN PUBLISHING, LTD. publication.

Samhain Publishing, Ltd.
512 Forest Lake Drive
Warner Robins, GA 31093
www.samhainpublishing.com

Joker's Wild: Three Nights
Copyright © 2007 by Lena Matthews
Print ISBN: 1-59998-724-4
Digital ISBN: 1-59998-163-7

Editing by Jessica Bimberg
Cover by Scott Carpenter

First Samhain Publishing, Ltd. electronic publication: November 2006
First Samhain Publishing, Ltd. print publication: August 2007

Dedication

This book is dedicated to the memory of Teri Smith. May your light shine in heaven as it did on earth.

Prologue

Twenty years earlier

Hunger, like most pain, could only be ignored for so long, but unlike the bruises on his back, the need to eat wouldn't disappear in a couple of days. Chris Davis was used to it though. After ten years of being raised by a strung-out mother and hyped up father, there wasn't much in the way of pain he hadn't experienced. But his stomach cramps weren't as imperative as the ache he could see shining from his little sister's dull brown eyes.

Octavia had become his only reason for staying home anymore, if you could call it home. Someone had to look after her, and although he knew he could survive with the Crips in the street, she never would be able to. He already did little things for D Dog to get money to take care of her, nothing that could get him busted or anything, just look-out stuff. He would never take the chance he would get locked up and leave her here, with them, alone.

Chris crept along the sticky carpeted floor very quietly, careful not to step on any squeaky floorboards in the rundown apartment building. He eased his way by his father who was passed out on the couch. Without turning on any lights, he slowly opened up the cabinet door, praying it wouldn't make a sound, and searched diligently for anything remotely resembling food. The bare cabinets were like screams of agony in his head.

Tears welled up behind his eyes, causing them to burn. But Chris fought to hold them back. Crying had never done him a lick of good in his entire life. It never stopped the blows from coming and it wouldn't put food in his sister's stomach. Closing the door as quietly as he had opened it, Chris debated what he should do next.

Just then, his mother stumbled into the apartment, flicking on the light as she passed through the doorway. She was dressed poorly, as usual, in a light green short skirt and purple top. Her hair once black, thick and full now stood on end, thin and graying. Her formerly beautiful dark brown face was now aged and scarred, gaunt with a layer of thick makeup. She, of course, thought she looked wonderful, but to Chris, she just looked plain sad. Ducking down low, Chris pressed his frail bruised back against the cabinet door and tried to get out of her line of vision. He would be punished for sure if they noticed him out of his room.

"What the hell is going on?" his father bellowed, getting up from the couch. There had been a time when Christopher Senior had been an attractive man, long before the war, and the heroin took a hold of him. Although it was before Chris had been born, he heard of it many times from his mother, who, of course, blamed his father for all of her problems.

Beverly leaned against the closed door with one hand wrapped around a bottle of Jack and the other in the hand of a man Chris had never seen before.

"Who the fuck is this?" his father demanded as he staggered to the doorway.

"This is a friend of mine." Beverly swayed unsteadily on her feet, pointing the bottle at the confused man. "Billy, meet Christopher, he's my 'usband but don't you worry none, you and me can still party."

"Woman, have you lost your mind?" Christopher pushed her against the door, and that was all Chris needed to see. Running low, he barely missed a swinging fist as he dove into his room, shutting the door behind him.

Octavia was curled up in the corner with an old rag doll held tightly in her hand. Her big brown eyes stood out in her small, pretty, mocha brown face. She was only five years old, and already she had the jaded look of pain etched into her features.

"What's going on?" she whispered from the corner, too afraid to move.

"Shh." Placing his finger across his lips, he motioned for her to be silent. The fight in the other room had escalated and he knew they were only moments away from bloodshed, or worse. Unlike other places, no one would call the police, not that they'd come there to the south side if they were called anyway. It was a sad lesson to learn so early in life. Not only did they not matter to their parents, they didn't matter to the state either. Just another poor black statistic in another poor black neighborhood.

The shouting grew louder, and something slammed against the door he was leaning against. Octavia jumped and huddled deeper in the corner, trying to make herself as small as possible.

The door flew open, knocking Chris over in the process. His mother stood in the doorway, bleeding and stoned.

"What did you do with my stuff?" she slurred.

"I don't know what you're talking about," he said, standing up.

Chris walked over some so Octavia was hidden from view behind him. He could tell by the way his mother was talking that this conversation would soon turn into a violent one. He was older and stronger, and much more equipped to take a blow from her than Octavia. And the sooner his mother erupted, the better.

Beverly was a hit and run kind of person. She only stayed long enough to do damage, then she would leave. That way she could pretend nothing happened and would have no reason to feel guilty the next day.

"I know you took my shit, you little bastard, and I want it back."

"I didn't take anything, Beverly," he denied, long past the time when he called her mother. "Maybe you already smoked it."

Beverly swung her arm hit him across the face, sending him to the ground. "You're jus' like your motherfucking father, always accusing me of something."

Standing over him, she seemed big and scary, but Chris wasn't afraid for himself, he was afraid for Octavia, who was whimpering in the corner.

"No, I'm not."

"Yes, you are," she screamed. "You ain't never going to be nobody and you ain't never going to go nowhere. You're nothing."

Chris just lay there and let her rage. He was no longer listening to what she had to say. He heard it all before. Breathing heavily, Beverly ran out of words to hurl at him and slammed out of the room.

To Chris' dismay the argument reared up again in the next room. Frightened, he wondered what he should do. She would be back, and if not her, then his dad. This night was only beginning.

Jumping up, Chris knew he had no other options. It was either stay there and hope they killed each other, or run and take Octavia out of there. Knowing the odds weren't in his favor that his parents might get a lucky shot off and take each other out, he pushed up the bedroom window, picked up his thin sister and put her out on the fire escape.

"Climb down, Tay," he urged, climbing out after her.

"I'm scared, Chris."

"I know, but we have to go." Grabbing her frail hand, he squeezed it gently and smiled reassuringly at her. "We're going to go get something to eat."

"But what if they come in and find we're gone?" Her eyes widened in fear.

"We'll deal with that tomorrow." Moving around her, Chris hurried down the stairs first, then stood watching nervously as Octavia climbed down slowly. She was so thin and it was really cold out there. He could feel her bones through her skin these days. Chris knew he had to do something fast, or she wouldn't survive another winter. They didn't have any winter clothes, and she got sick so easily.

As she finally reached the bottom, they walked quickly out the alleyway. Chris made sure Octavia stayed behind him. Gripping her hand tightly, he walked by people passed out on the street, and with signs begging for money saying "God Bless". Everyone talked about God in the ghetto. Between sips of whiskey and drags off pipes, the local preacher man warned of God and his retribution to those who sinned.

His dad would just laugh and tell him that there was no God, but Chris knew differently. There had to be a God. Even as cynical and as young as he was, Chris truly believed there was a place good people went and a place bad people went. He knew for sure there was a heaven, because they were living in hell.

When he turned the corner, Chris spotted two young black men standing on the corner laughing, in thick coats and gold chains. The taller of the two saw Chris and waved him over.

"Hey, little man, what you doing out so late?"

Walking to them, he looked the ringleader in the eye and stared back. You didn't punk out in this neighborhood. You either came real, or died real quick. Many people in the neighborhood were scared of D Dog, but Chris was too naïve and too tired to be. "My sister needs some food, and we need a place to stay."

"Oh yeah?" he asked, looking down at Octavia.

"Yes." Chris pulled her behind him, blocking her from D's view. "You got a job for me?"

"Of course I do," he said, his dark eyes shining in the moonlight. "But first things first, let's take care of your sister."

People wondered why kids got involved in gangs. Most thought it was for power and respect, but Chris knew differently. Sometimes it was better to go with the devil you know than the devil you didn't. And if the devil you knew provided you with food and clothes, then how evil was he after all?

With a nod of his head, Chris followed them to the car parked across the street and got in with Octavia. The warm air trickled from the front seat to the back, where Octavia huddled against his side.

"Where we going, Chris?" she whispered drowsily.

"Someplace warm, Tay," he whispered back. As she drifted off to sleep with her head on his lap, Chris thought back to what his mother had said. He wasn't like his

13

father, he thought angrily, and he never would be. He wasn't like either one of them and he'd prove it.

Chapter One

Chris awoke from his nightmare, wet from sweat. It had been a long time since he'd had a dream about his father, and it was humiliating to know a dead man still possessed so much power over him.

Tossing the soaked sheets back, Chris rolled over and sat up with his feet over the side of the bed. Agitated, he shook his head to clear his mind. Still shaky, he remembered visions of his childhood, of loud screams and hard hits, vivid again because of his dream.

Chris liked to refer to that time as the "Before Years". Before he and Octavia had been taken in by the Wilsons and given a better life. He tried to squash thoughts of the nightmare from his mind as he got up and walked down the hall of his three-bedroom home.

He entered his kitchen, took a glass out of his cabinet and filled it with cold water from the dispenser on the refrigerator. Drinking half the glass in one swallow, Chris leaned against the door and ran the cool glass against his warm brown head. Breathing in deep and slow, he tried to relax and calm his racing pulse. He drained the glass, washed it out in the sink and left it on the counter. Walking back down the hall, he headed through his bedroom to the bathroom.

Going into the bathroom, Chris turned on the light and started a shower. The large bathroom warmed under the hot track lighting. The caramel colored walls lent a soothing tone to the masculine room. No flowery pictures on the walls, his bathroom was one of the many safe havens in his home.

After growing up with nothing, Chris treasured cleanliness and expensive items. His bathroom had both. A stereo was installed into the wall across from his sink and was filled with an eclectic range of music. From early rap like Run D.M.C. to classic Motown. Today though, he was in the mood for a little Miles Davis to go with his shower.

On rare nights like tonight, the only thing that could wash off the filth of his childhood was a long shower, a stiff drink and a hard screw. Seeing how he woke up alone, he guessed he'd have to settle for the first two.

Dropping his cotton boxers on the ground, Chris slid behind the dark chocolate shower curtain and stepped under the hot spray. Water splattered against his smooth shaven head as he lathered up, washing the horrible memories away with the sweat. His hand soaped his well-defined body, fine-tuned from years at the gym.

He had learned early on that the best defense was a quick offense, and of course a good right hook. Papa Wilson had enrolled him in boxing soon after he was placed with them, to help Chris work off some of his anger. His anger didn't recede, but he learned a valuable lesson from boxing. It's not about who hits the hardest, it's about who hits who the fastest.

Turning off the water, he grabbed the auburn colored cotton towel off the rack and briskly rubbed his body, looping it around his neck when he was done. Grabbing a second towel, he wrapped it around his waist and walked out his steaming bathroom. Looking over at his nightstand, Chris noticed the time. It was after four so he might as well stay up, he thought with disgust. He needed to do something to clear his head and work off some of this restless energy. Putting on his running shorts and a T-shirt, Chris prepared to go for a run.

Although he lived in a good neighborhood, Chris always locked his door and ran with his license. Police were police in every state, and a black man running down the street, even dressed as he was, should always be prepared to be questioned. It wasn't right but it was life, the crappy part, but life nevertheless.

The neighborhood was quiet and still dark as he let himself out his home. Chris sat down on the moist grass and stretched out, relaxing his body and his mind for his jog. The peaceful silence was a vast contrast to the loud boisterous neighborhood he grew up in. Dogs barking in the background were a refreshing change from screaming husbands and crying babies.

Jogging out his yard, he headed down the street. His feet pounded against the pavement, and he ran to a beat in his head. Setting his own rhythm, Chris picked up his speed, determined to erase all images of his nightmare from his mind.

The sky began to lighten, and a slight chill filled the air. The cold morning breeze penetrated his aching lungs, which burned from his pace. He wasn't really equipped to run as fast and as far as he was, but still he ran, pumping his arms and slamming his feet as he went.

Chris pushed himself, testing his limits to see how much he could take. His blood was pumping, and he began to breathe harder, but then the adrenaline rush kicked in, sending a euphoric high through his blood stream. Chris continued running until the pain in his lungs blended with the pain in his legs, forcing him to stop. Bending over, he rested his hands on his knees as he gasped for breath. It might not be as fun as sex, but pushing himself to the limit was as close as he was going to get today.

Looking down at his watch, Chris noted the time. He turned around and began to walk slowly back, building up his energy until he could once again run. Taking off slowly this time, he eased himself into a more comfortable steady rhythm.

Entering his block, he nodded to the few neighbors who were walking to their cars, and jogged to his door. He had time for another quick shower and a light breakfast before he had to head off to work. Dropping his keys on his entryway table, Chris headed down the hall to his bathroom.

Two hours later, Chris walked into his office ready to face the day. The morning jog had done its job of clearing his mind. His bad dream, like his childhood, was a thing of the past. Smiling at the few employees in his outer office, Chris walked past his secretary's desk, empty for once, and strolled into his office.

Chris tried to make his office as comfortable as his home, since he spent more time there than at his place. Growing up poor instilled a need to achieve financial security for himself as well as his sister, so neither one of them ever had to worry about money again. It also inspired him to surround himself with beautiful things.

Tastefully decorated, his office presented a warm and soothing appearance. His large oak desk dominated the room, surrounded by plants and a few authentic African sculptures. A suede loveseat filled one corner next to his built-in bookshelf. Two brown leather chairs were angled towards his desk. His office window faced the street, but allowed him to witness the sun fading from the sky every evening. He was a lucky man, and he knew it.

After graduating at the top of his class, he worked hard to save up enough money to open his own company. He and his college roommate, Dylan Thompson, had opened up their own financing company three years ago, and they were now beginning to reap the rewards. Their hard work and reputation for being fair and dedicated people helped to build their business up, and after awhile, they actually began to turn down clients because of lack of time.

He hired a new secretary a few months ago, after his previous assistant had taken maternity leave. Eliza was supposed to be a temp, but Ellen decided not to return, leaving him no other choice but to replace her.

It wasn't as if hiring Eliza had been a completely bad idea. She was extremely competent, always at work on time, dependable. Another big plus was she wasn't bitchy like Mrs. Howard, Dylan's secretary, but she did have one major strike against her. He was extremely attracted to her. More so to her than any other woman he had met in a really long time.

Not only was she beautiful, but she also had a body to die for. She was around five foot seven inches tall, with long jet-black hair and big, beautiful emerald green eyes. Her lightly tan skin hinted at her Puerto Rican heritage, as did her soft, lyrical, accented voice. She had a way of rolling her R's that always had him salivating. Her voice, like her body, kept him awake at night.

Chris had to stop himself on a daily basis from turning into the lecherous stereotypical boss chasing her around the office. As of late, he began to feel their attraction was a mutual thing, which wasn't good for his business or for him.

He didn't know a lot about her because Eliza mainly kept to herself. She was a hard worker, made great coffee and never complained about staying late. Her ring finger was bare, but these days that wasn't as telling as it used to be, and because of company policy there weren't any pictures on her desk of family and friends. She was almost as much of an enigma as she was beautiful.

Lost in thought, he was oblivious to Eliza standing in the doorway until he faintly caught her scent on the recycled air. Her aroma was a mixture of something exotic, arousing and very feminine all at the same time. It was a smell that drove him insane. Looking up, he watched her as she approached.

"Good morning," she said, walking towards him with a steaming cup of coffee.

"Morning," he replied back huskily. As usual, she looked fucking great. Eliza strolled up to him with a come hither smile and her eyes seemed deeper than they really should have been.

Dressed in a black knee length skirt and ivory colored buttoned up blouse, she dangerously straddled the line of professionalism and eroticism. The buttons on her shirt were not fastened all the way to the top, stopping just a button away from the top of her breasts, exposing her bountiful cleavage. Her skirt, although knee length, tightly molded her curvy figure. She made him want to bend her over his desk and take a bite out of her full ass, and tongue her nipples until they were hard enough to cut glass. Just thinking of all the nasty things he could do to her made his penis jump in anticipation. He was going to fuck her if it was the last thing he did.

Standing next to him, she looked down as she handed him his coffee. Her green eyes twinkled with merriment, as if she knew where his hands wanted to go.

"There were several messages on the machine this morning."

"Any I need to know about?"

"Yes, Mr. Kincaid called…"

"No," Chris said firmly.

"You didn't even let me finish the message."

He reached up for his coffee as she pulled it out of his reach.

"People are going to think you're a hard ass if you don't watch it."

"And I would care why?"

"Come on, Chris, it's for charity," she cajoled. "What's one night? You buy a dinner, you donate money, you leave."

"Because," he said, reaching up for his coffee again, "it's never that simple with those people. It's shake this and kiss that. I'll just send a check and call it a day."

"I bet you're worried you won't find a date," Eliza leaned against his desk, placing his coffee behind her out of his reach. "If you beg me nicely, I'll go with you."

Raising one brow, Chris said haughtily, "I assure you, Eliza, getting a date has never been a problem for me."

"Color me surprised," Eliza teased. "It must be your charming personality, because it can't be your good looks."

"You find something," he paused, looking for the right word, "amiss with my looks?"

"Of course I do. I make it a rule to never go out with a man prettier than I am." Chris flushed at her compliment, causing Eliza to laugh.

She was such a damn flirt, he thought irately. No matter how hard he tried to be serious when around her, she was always trying to make him smile or laugh. Eliza straightened and picked up his coffee, handing it to him.

"It isn't possible for me or anyone else to be prettier than you," he replied, reaching up for his coffee. Their fingers brushed each other's, neither one pulling away, allowing their touch to linger longer than necessary. He could tell he had surprised her with his comment. She looked at him thoughtfully and he stared back. The moment was broken by a phone ringing in the outer office. "Do I have a busy day?"

"It depends."

"On what?"

"If Dylan snaps out of his funk or not."

"Fuck," Chris muttered, setting his untouched coffee down. Dylan and his girlfriend Kayla had gotten into a little disagreement a week or so ago, and ever since, he had been pure hell to work with. Walking around the office like someone killed his dog, Dylan had been unfocused, unreliable and completely annoying. "I'm going to have to talk to him again, aren't I?"

"Would that be so bad?" she teased.

"Of course it would," he frowned. "I'm a guy. We don't talk. We hit things. Big things. Things that hopefully will swing back."

"And does that help? Hitting something?" Cocking her head to the side, Eliza folded her arms across her breasts.

"Well," he tilted his head thinking, "only if it bleeds."

"See, that's what's wrong with the world today," she said, raising her delicately arched eyebrow. Leaning forward, she grasped his arm, feeling his biceps. "This here always gets them into trouble. Men act first, talk later."

He caught her hand and held it against him. His hard, callused hand lay against her smooth, satiny flesh. Running his fingers lightly against the back of hers, he looked up into her eyes. Eliza's smile was frozen on her face, and her breath deepened.

"We can talk before or after," he said softly. The mood automatically changed as the sexual tension filled the air. The atmosphere seemed heavier, thicker with desire.

Staring at each other, they both jumped as the phone rang again, interrupting their interlude. He had never been as tempted as he was now to take control of her. He could tell the attraction was mutual by the way her eyes seemed to glaze over and her breasts began to rise. Chris secretly wondered what might have happened if the phone hadn't rung. Whoever said "saved by the bell", apparently hadn't been this close to heaven.

Eliza leaned over his oak desk, bent forward and picked up his phone, giving him a perfect shot of her cleavage. An arousing image popped in his head of him holding her full globes with his large hands as he pumped his hard cock between them.

"Thomas and Wilson Financing Company, how can I help you?" Eliza's sensual voice broke the spell his mind had woven around him. Chris looked up at her and noticed the slightly amused look on her face.

The sparkle in her eyes alerted Chris to the fact she knew where his eyes had been gazing, and maybe even where his thoughts had wandered. Chris flushed in embarrassment. He had just been caught red-handed, staring at her chest. Glancing back down at his desk, he shuffled random papers, pretending to be occupied.

He mentally cursed himself for his blunder. If he didn't watch it, he was going to either wind up fighting a half a million-dollar lawsuit or above her, pounding into her wet flesh. Either way, he would be fucked.

"Please hold." Hitting the hold button on his phone, Eliza hung the phone up and stood back up. Sliding her hand across his desk from the phone to her hip, she watched him as he watched her. "It's Michael Lundy, from Barron's. He wants to make an appointment."

"Do we have any openings today?" he asked, looking her in the eyes.

"I'll check." Turning away, Eliza strolled from across his office and paused at the door. Laying her hand against the doorframe, she looked back over her shoulder at him. "I'm not a big talker afterwards, but during is another story."

Chris's mouth fell open in shock at her statement. He wasn't used to being around anyone so comfortable with their sexuality. He was used to women playing coy and pretending not to want a man, not someone who was so open. An urge like he never felt before began to well up inside of him.

There was no doubt in his mind they would be fucking soon. It was only a matter of time.

Chapter Two

Eliza rolled over as her alarm went off, hitting it feebly with her flopping hand. Seven o'clock kept coming earlier and earlier every day. Stretching under her quilt, she wiggled her toes against the soft sheets and slowly opened her eyes. Another night of erotic dreams featuring her favorite late night star, Chris. At the rate she was going, she'd burst from sexual frustration before he ever made a move.

At first she thought he was just being gentlemanly about it, which was fine with her. But after six months of heated looks and slight caresses, if he didn't do something fast, she was going to straddle him in his chair and ride him for all he was worth.

Thinking of the image of her straddling him, Eliza smiled as she imagined the look on his face. Sometimes he could seem so cold, and other times he was as open as a book. Chris had a very dry sense of humor that always managed to make her smile. It was one of the reasons she agreed to stay on with him at his company. She wanted to work somewhere that was actually a pleasure to be at, not someplace she would dread going every day.

Closing her eyes, she thought of Chris and wondered—not for the first time—what kind of lover he would be. Eliza had only been with two men in her life. The first was her high school boyfriend, whom she fumbled around with in the back of his car. As nervous and as inept as they were, she was surprised they had even managed to complete the act.

The second was her ex-husband, Javier, who left a lot to be desired. It wasn't as if he were a bad lover, he just wasn't very giving. In the last two years, she had learned more about her body, experimenting alone, than she had the entire time she was with him. The best part of Javier was asleep in the other room.

Running her hand under her nightshirt, she thought back to Chris, to his large firm hands. Cupping her breasts, she teased her nipples to hard peaks, gently tugging on them as she imagined Chris taking her full breasts into his mouth. His dark hands squeezing and tonguing her heavy mounds as he ground into her.

Releasing one of her breasts, she slid her hand down her flat stomach and into her red cotton panties. Her fingers feathered lightly across her bare mound as she envisioned him dropping down in front of her and taking her aching clit into his mouth. His bald head between her thighs, his tongue lapping up her sweet nectar. Shuddering at the image, she slid her fingers between her lips and fingered her wet opening.

Skimming her clit slowly, she gently rubbed her taut bud in small circles, widening her movements, increasing her speed. Her body stiffened as she sped up her fingers, rubbing against her clit as she squeezed her erect nipple with her other hand. Eliza pictured Chris plunging into her, his hard cock pounding her mercilessly until she came.

Her body rocked with pleasure as she arched off the bed, erupting in unison with her fantasy. Biting back her moan, Eliza shook from the power of her release as she rode out the wave of pleasure cruising through her body.

Panting, she lay back on the bed and slid her hand from underneath her underwear. These morning sessions of masturbation had become routine since she began working for Chris. With an inquisitive child like Jocelyn, Eliza was uncomfortable having toys around, and at the rate she was going, she would be crippled from carpel tunnel long before Chris made a move.

"Chris..." she whispered softly, visions of him floating like sugarplums in her head. It should be illegal to be so attractive.

Still aroused, she ran her damp fingers up over her stomach and across her breasts. Her nipples were still hard, and she contemplated going back for seconds. Moving her fingers down, she cursed as the phone rang. Yanking her hands from under her nightshirt, she wiped her damp fingers on her shirt and reached shakily for the phone.

"Morning," she answered, her voice husky from her arousal.

"Did I interrupt something?" Veronica, her sister-in-law, asked.

Chuckling softly, she said "I wish, but no, I'm in bed alone."

"Late night dreams about the boss."

"Yes," she sighed dreamily.

"Why don't you just attack the man and take him home with you?"

"Because it's still against the law to kidnap men, even handsome men."

"Tell me about this dreamboat boss man of yours I keep hearing so much about."

"Think of Vin Diesel but make him darker and sexier."

"Sexier than Vin?" Veronica asked, drooling into the phone.

"Nice deep gravelly voice, well defined body, luscious lips and his ass..."

"Yes," Veronica begged. "What about it?"

"Sonnets were written about his ass." Rolling on her side, Eliza chuckled as Veronica moaned in mock despair.

"This is working for me."

"It better not be. You're eight months pregnant with my future nephew," Eliza kidded.

"I'm pregnant girl, not dead."

Laughing, Eliza said, "Ain't that the truth?"

Her bedroom door started creaking open, and Jocelyn peered around the opened door. "You up, Mom?"

"Yes, honey," she said, lifting her head up and smiling at her. "I'll call you after I take Jocelyn to the doctor," she said into the phone as Jocelyn ran over and jumped on the bed.

"Later."

Hanging up the phone, she pulled Jocelyn down onto the bed and gave her a big hug. Leaning her head over, she inhaled the sweet powdery sent of her daughter, and her heart filled with joy.

Half listening to Jocelyn as she chatted about her morning cartoons, Eliza sighed to herself as she reflected back on her morning. Coming was a great way to start the day, but it would have been a lot better if Chris were inside of her, instead of her fingers.

After Jocelyn's check-up, Eliza took her to the park as a reward. It was a beautiful day, too beautiful to be stuck inside, and she wanted to spend the day with her girl under the bright sunny sky. Walking on the trail, they headed towards a bench facing the play area. Eliza smiled politely at the woman who scooted over so they could sit down, and took out her "mom kit" full of first aid and goodies.

Lathering up Jocelyn with sun block, she glanced over at the woman and tried to place her face. Recognition came almost immediately. It was Kayla Martin, her other boss Dylan's girlfriend. She had seen her around the office on several occasions and had even talked to her on the phone. The sad expression on Kayla's face made Eliza wonder if she was feeling down for the same reason Dylan was.

Sending Jocelyn off to play, she turned to Kayla and asked, "You don't recognize me, do you?"

"No," she replied softly. "But you look familiar."

"I work for your friend, Dylan," she said, smiling and offering her hand. "We've talked several times on the phone and I've seen you in the office, but I don't think we've been formally introduced. I'm Eliza Rivera."

"Oh, hi." Taking her hand, Kayla shook it before gesturing towards Jocelyn. "I didn't know you had a little girl. She's a beauty."

"Thanks." Smiling, Eliza looked over at Jocelyn climbing the ladder to the slide. "Jocelyn is a joy."

They sat in silence for a while as Eliza tried to think of something to say to cheer up the obviously depressed woman. Reaching into her magic mom bag, she pulled out Jocelyn's favorite treat, gummy worms, and offered one to Kayla. Although it wasn't chocolate, it was still candy, and it was the best silence breaker she had.

Kayla took the treat as tears trickled down her face. Eliza's heart immediately went to the other woman. Growing up with three older brothers, she wasn't known for her ability to communicate without screaming, punching or biting, but something inside her urged her to reach out to Kayla.

"Want to talk about it?" Eliza asked softly.

"No."

"Does it have anything to do with my gloomy-looking boss?"

"No," she denied. Then, looking over at Eliza hopefully, she asked, "He's been gloomy?"

Smiling, Eliza nodded. "Never seen such a whipped puppy in my life. Even the dragon lady is being nice to him."

A ghost of a smile flickered across her face before she said, "I just came from the bank."

"Hell, I'd be crying too," Eliza joked, trying to cheer her up.

Kayla flashed her grin again, and continued, "I was turned down for a loan for my Wand."

Eliza wasn't sure what Kayla was talking about. Whatever the Wand was, it was apparent that it was important to her. "I'm sorry to hear that."

"Yeah, me too, but the worst part is, it was all for nothing."

"What?"

"The disagreement Dylan and I had, all for nothing." Sadness filled the woman's face as she remarked, "No Wand, no Dylan, no real reason for us to not be talking anymore, and I'm sure Dylan is somewhere laughing his ass off."

Completely confused, Eliza tried to decipher the information Kayla had shared. She had no idea what a bank loan, a Wand and Dylan had to do with each other. It was like missing the punch line in a bawdy joke. None of it made sense, so she went with the Dylan comment since it was the only thing she recognized in Kayla's entire speech.

"I'm sure that's not the case," she said sympathetically. "He hasn't looked like he's been laughing in awhile."

"It doesn't matter. None of it does." Glumly she turned to Eliza and smiled sadly again. "Thanks for listening to me whine, and for the gummy worm."

Eliza watched Kayla walk away, thinking back to how sad Dylan had looked lately. She had never seen two people so obviously in love and so completely miserable, in her entire life. Always making it a point to never butt into other people's business, she wasn't sure what she should do. Part of her wanted to run after Kayla and hug her. The maternal instinct to do so was really hard to ignore, but the other part knew she should just mind her own business. Never one to sit back and watch people suffer needlessly, Eliza gathered her and Jocelyn's stuff and called to the playing little girl.

"Come on, Mami, we have to go."

"But we just got here, Momma," she pouted.

Running her hand down the side of Jocelyn's face, Eliza smiled and said, "I know, Mami, but we'll come back. I have to stop by my job for a minute."

"You said you had today off."

Sighing in frustration, Eliza put her hands on her hips. "I do, I just have to run by really quickly. We won't be long, and we'll go for ice cream afterwards."

Smiling, Jocelyn grabbed her mother's hand and started pulling her towards the car. Laughing, Eliza shook her head, and was once again amazed at the way kids minds worked.

The drive to the office took less than five minutes, and Jocelyn chatted up a storm in the backseat. The quick drive hadn't given her time to formulate a plan yet, but she figured she could wing it. She was a mom after all. She was used to thinking on her feet. Getting out of the car, Jocelyn had her Dora the Explorer backpack in her hand. It carried all of her coloring books and crayons.

"I don't plan to be here that long," joked Eliza.

"It's for just in case, Momma," Jocelyn implored.

"Okay," smiled Eliza. "Just in case" had become Jocelyn's new catch phrase. Everything now was "just in case". The two walked into the air-conditioned building and sighed appreciatively. Their car didn't have any, so it was a refreshing change to be somewhere that did.

Walking over to her desk, Eliza picked up Jocelyn and set her in the chair. Looking into Chris's empty office, she hesitated. Not wanting to leave Jocelyn there without talking it over with him, she debated on what to do. Thinking she'd just be a minute, Eliza decided it would be okay just this once.

"Sit here, Mami, don't touch anything," she said sternly. "I'll be back in a couple of minutes."

"Okay," she replied, opening up her backpack and getting out her coloring book. Eliza looked down at her bent head and at Chris's empty office one more time before heading down the hallway to Dylan's office.

Chris rounded the corner just as Eliza disappeared into Dylan's office and nodded at Mrs. Howard. Strolling down the hall, he stopped short when he saw a little girl sitting at Eliza's desk. It was such a surprise that for a moment Chris wondered if he was seeing things when she turned towards him and smiled. He automatically smiled back, which amazed him. Not one to spend time with kids, Chris was a little apprehensive about what to say to her.

"Hi."

"Well, hello yourself," he said, coming around the desk. He sat down on the corner of the desk and looked down at her. She was a pretty little thing, with a head full of chocolate colored curls. She had the biggest green eyes he had ever seen and a cute pug nose. She smiled at him, showing a space between her bottom teeth, where it looked like she had lost a tooth recently. Her smile seemed vaguely familiar. "Are you here with someone?"

"Uh huh." She nodded, looking back at down at her coloring book. "Do you want to color with me? You can color Benny the Bull, I don't gots that color blue, but you can use this one." She held up a bright blue crayon for him.

"No, that's okay." Looking around the office, Chris wondered whom this little imp belonged to. "What's your name, sweetheart?" he asked in a soothing tone. The last thing he wanted to do was to scare her and cause her to cry. He never was any good with crying girls, not even Octavia.

"Jocelyn."

"That's a really pretty name. Do you know where your mommy or daddy is?"

"My mom went that away. She told me to stay here and not to touch anything. We're going to go get ice cream later. Do you want to come?"

"No, that's okay." Leaning back a little, Chris looked down the hall towards Dylan's office, trying to catch a glimpse of Jocelyn's mom. "Do you know what your mommy's name is?"

Frowning up at him, she replied, "Of course I do. I'm little, not stupid."

Chris burst out laughing at her remark. It had been a long time since he had been a kid, but he could still remember hating the way adults talked to him as if he were simple. "I'm sorry, Princess Jocelyn." He bowed his head regally, causing her to smile. "How silly of me. Will Your Royal Highness do me the honor of telling me your mother's name?"

Giggling, she placed her hand over her mouth to stifle the sound. Her green eyes sparkled from laughter behind her dark lashes. Chris smiled at the sound, amazed to hear something so simple and lyrical from something so small and pretty.

Putting her hand down, Jocelyn smiled up at him. "My mom's name is Eliza Marie Rivera and I'm Jocelyn Anna Rivera and I'm five."

The smile on his face froze as the name came out of her mouth. Eliza had a kid. How the hell was this possible? A cute kid, but a kid nevertheless. Disappointment like he'd never known froze him as he stared down at a kid he would never have, born to a woman he could no longer have. The "no kid" rule was an important one for him.

"What's your name?" Jocelyn asked, interrupting his thoughts.

"Chris," he said from between clenched teeth.

"That's a nice name," she said smiling. "We have a Chris in my class, but he's not very nice, he's always in time out. Do you have to go to time out a lot?"

"No, but I'm sure sometimes I need to."

Jocelyn giggled, a sweet soft sound that forced a smile from his tightened lips. Chris had forgotten how wonderful kids could sound. Not that he and Octavia had a lot to laugh about as kids, but there were times they did, and it was a wonderful sound.

Looking up, Chris saw Eliza walking towards them with a smile on her face. Now looking at both of them, he could see the resemblance clearly. Jocelyn was going to be just as beautiful as her mother when she got older, a heartbreaker in training.

Standing up, Chris dropped the smile from his face, hiding behind the wall of indifference he had used as a shield for so long. He noticed the look of surprise on Eliza's face at the change in his demeanor, but quickly forced himself not to care about her feelings.

"I see you met my daughter." Placing her hand lovingly on Jocelyn's shoulder, she smiled up at him.

"Yes," he replied coldly. "I was unaware I had hired a new secretary."

Annoyance flashed across her face at his remark. Her body stiffened and Chris wanted to kick himself for causing her to tense up, but it was for her own good.

"Sorry, Mr. Wilson," she said rigidly. "It won't happen again."

Nodding firmly, he backed away from her desk. Part of him wanted to take back his harsh words, to tell her he thought she had a great kid. He wanted to know about Jocelyn's father, to know anything about her he didn't know, but he didn't have that right.

"Time to go, Mami," she said, gathering Jocelyn's things together on her desk. Chris watched her, eyeing her angry movements. He briefly wondered if she would take out her anger on Jocelyn before he reminded himself not all mothers were like his.

"Bye, Mr. Chris," Jocelyn said, looking up at him.

Lightly smiling down at her, he replied, "Bye, kid." Before he could stop himself, he reached out his hand and rustled her soft curly hair.

Looking up from her, Chris eyed Eliza in disappointment before turning and going into his office.

He saw the confused look in Eliza's eyes at his hot and cold personality.

Chapter Three

Shutting down her computer, Eliza counted the minutes until she could escape into a hot bath. It had been a long day. Hell, it had been a long two weeks. Her relationship with Chris at work was very strained with neither one really talking to the other, unless it had to do with work. The comfortable atmosphere she had loved so much had disappeared as soon as he had met Jocelyn.

It was a big surprise to find out Chris didn't like kids, but that was the only way she could explain his actions. Being a mom was her first priority so she refused to even imagine a future with him anymore. Jocelyn had told her he was really nice and funny, so Eliza didn't understand his instant attitude.

Her intercom buzzed. "Eliza, I want to dictate a letter to you before you leave."

Sighing, she grumbled under her breath. Of course he wanted her to type something up. It was ten minutes to closing. Whatever made her think she could actually leave on time?

"I'll be right in," she replied into the intercom. Taking her pad and pen off her desk, she pushed back her chair grumpily. She wanted to channel Jocelyn and throw a fit and stomp into his office, but thought better of it. The quicker she went in there and took his dictation, the quicker she could leave.

Eliza walked briskly into his office, pulled back a chair and sat in it stiffly. Crossing her legs, she looked over at him and waited for him to begin. If he noticed her displeasure, he ignored it and just sat back in his chair.

He had begun to look a little tired to her, but she didn't feel it was her place anymore to inquire. Not that it ever was, but a few weeks ago, she would have been comfortable teasing him, now she just felt as if she were a bother.

The tension between them was noticeable, but they ignored it as he dictated his letter. She re-crossed her legs and looked up when he paused in mid-sentence. He was staring at the split on the side of her soft gray skirt. The way she had her legs positioned, the split showed the top of her thigh high stocking. Smiling to herself, Eliza was happy to see she could still affect him. Lowering the pen down to the side of the split, she tapped it lightly against the opening, startling him into looking up.

As he stared at her, she tilted her head to the side and gave him an inviting look. "You were saying?" she asked huskily.

"I...umm..." Clearing his throat, he picked back up where he had left off.

But it didn't matter to Eliza, she knew he was still as interested in her as he was two weeks ago. He still wanted her. Of that she was sure.

Finishing up, she asked, "Is that all, sir?"

"Yes," he said, shifted his gaze from his notes back to her. "Oh, and Eliza, do me a favor."

"Sir?"

"Can this sir bullshit, it's not you and it's annoying me."

"Yes, sir." She saluted him with her pad and turned back to the door.

"Smart ass," she heard him grumble as she shut his door.

Walking to her desk, she sat down and typed his letter. Pounding on the keys in her frustration, she pretended each key was his head, his stubborn pigheaded head. When she finished the letter, Eliza printed it out. She wanted to get out of there before he came back out and said something else to piss her off. As the paper ejected from the printer, she reached down and grabbed it. Standing up, she came face to face with Kayla. Dressed in a bright yellow shirt and torn jeans, Kayla had her hair in two pigtails and a huge grin on her face.

Eliza couldn't help smiling at the other woman. No one could stay mad looking at a shirt that bright. "Hello."

"Just the woman I wanted to see." Kayla came around the desk and plopped on it, grinning widely.

"Really, great." Eliza said, sitting back in her chair. "Why?"

Kicking her feet back and forth against the cabinet, she replied, "Dylan said you play poker, and I wanted to invite you to our game tonight."

"Well, did he happen to mention I blackmailed him? Because that's probably the only reason he asked you to invite me."

"No, he didn't," Kayla answered, intrigued. "Blackmail... Umm do I even want to know?"

"Do you still want to love him tomorrow?" Eliza teased

"Yes."

"Then don't ask."

"Great." Kayla laughed. "Well, no, he didn't mention that, but don't worry, I will."

Chris walked out of his office just as Kayla laughed. Seeing her, his stern face lit up. "Hey, Professor, what brings you here?"

Hopping off the desk, Kayla walked over to him and gave him a big hug. "Just dropping by to pick up Dylan. We're stopping by the jewelry store to pick up my ring."

"Was something wrong with it?" he inquired.

"Nope, I just want it really sparkly for tonight." Wiggling her brows up and down, Kayla teased, "I'm going to use the sparkle to distract you men."

"I'm not falling for that this time, woman." Chris tapped Kayla lightly on her pert nose. "So keep that diamond and those boobs out of my line of vision. Dylan told me what you did last time."

Eliza sat back and watched the interplay between them, beginning to get upset. She hadn't seen Chris so relaxed and happy in awhile, and although she liked Kayla, if she touched Chris one more time, Eliza was going to knock her on her ass. Eliza stood up stiffly and grabbed her black purse from her desk, flinching as she heard Chris laughing again.

"I'll be back," Chris said, walking back into his office.

Turning back to Eliza, Kayla asked, "Well, can I expect to see you tonight?"

"I don't know," she hedged, looking over her shoulder at Chris bent over his desk. "I don't think it's a good idea. Chris isn't actually my biggest fan right now."

"Well, great," Kayla kidded. "That man is ruthless. I've got a wedding to pay for, and I need all the distraction I can get."

Laughing, Eliza agreed, "All right, give me your address and I'll stop by."

"Great." Bending over, Kayla wrote down her address. "We girls have to stick together."

Chris picked through the mixed nuts in the can, trying his best to ignore his rumbling stomach. They were waiting for the pizza to be delivered for the poker game so they could chow. But for now, he would have to make due with the scraps of food he could scrounge up himself.

Looking around Dylan and Kayla's apartment Chris could definitely tell their stuff apart. They had just moved in together and although he thought Dylan and Kayla were a great match for each other, he wasn't so sure about their stuff. It didn't seem to blend together as well as the lovebirds. They had different tastes and different styles. It was easy to tell what belonged to whom, especially when it was souvenir cups from Burger King, which Chris knew had to be Kayla's, and Lenox dishes from Dillard's.

Although they had different tastes, Chris thought Dylan and Kayla would make out okay. He had never seen Dylan as happy as he was with Kayla. And after working with him the last couple of months, Chris had decided if they ever broke up again, he would just close the business and take up fishing, because Dylan had been damn near impossible to work with. He had been completely miserable and there was nothing worse than working with someone who was so damn down. Chris kept expecting to walk into work and hear Dylan listening to Barry Manilow, or some other weepy crap.

Even their poker game was different, he thought, a bit disgruntled. Instead of the usual guys, Kayla said she invited two of her friends to play. So much for belching and telling lies. It was one thing to play with Kayla. She was just one of the guys, she was used to them. But to be infiltrated by two more women, that was just asking for trouble.

Not that he thought women couldn't play a good game of poker. Kayla had won three months ago after all, but he was afraid the conversation would end up on periods and hairstyles. And if one person brought up the wedding, he was out of there. It was bad enough he had to be in the damn thing, but to have to sit and talk about colors and invitations was more than a guy could handle.

The doorbell ringing brought him out of his daze. Sitting the peanut can on the counter next to the cards, he took his wallet out of his back pocket, and opened the door. "It's about ti—"

Eliza stood in the doorway, looking extremely hot. Dressed in a light violet summer dress, the sight of her made his mouth water. She had her beautiful midnight black hair pulled up so her long graceful light brown neck was exposed. The way her tresses were styled begged for him to pull them loose and run them all over his body.

"Can I come in?" she questioned, looking amused.

Stepping back, he moved out of the way so she could enter the apartment. "What are you doing here?" he asked ungraciously.

"I was invited to the game."

"Don't you mean you blackmailed an invitation?"

"No." Her smile dropped and her tone changed, expressing her irritation. "Kayla came by the office and personally invited me."

"Look, if you're that hard up for money, maybe you should consider a second job."

"Look, Chris, I may work for you, but on my off time, I'm my own boss."

"Who's with your kid?" he asked rudely. Chris could tell it was the wrong thing to say by the way she went still and looked at him.

"She has a name." Eliza reminded him angrily. "*Jocelyn* is with my mother."

"Don't you think you should be home with her?"

"I am allowed a night out every once in awhile," she said, putting her hands on her hips. Walking up behind them, Kayla interrupted their argument as she greeted Eliza.

"I'm glad you could make it," Kayla said, smiling at Eliza. Kayla briefly hugged her as if they were old friends. When did they get so freaking close, he wondered.

"Well, at least someone is happy I came," she remarked, staring at Chris.

The tension was very noticeable, causing Kayla to glance quickly between them. "Can I get you a drink?" she asked, breaking the awkward silence. "Now we're just waiting for Scott and then the games can begin."

"I'll do it," offered Chris, looking for any excuse to bail. He needed to get away from Eliza before he said or did something he'd regret, like slipping up her shirt and tonguing her erect nipple. She was driving him crazy. It was hard enough having to work with her every day, but he couldn't even get away from her on his free time. Walking back into the kitchen area, Chris struggled to get himself under control.

Ever since he found out Eliza had a kid, he'd completely backed off, immediately placing her in the "couldn't have" column. Chris tried his damnedest to push her away, but Eliza was a hard woman to get rid of. It was almost like she was in heat. He could fucking smell her essence. Hell, he was even tempted to ask her if she dipped her finger in her cunt and dabbed it behind her ears as perfume. She smelled that fucking good.

Opening the refrigerator door, Chris stood in front of it, trying to cool off. Just talking to her had him all hot and bothered. She was like a walking, talking wet dream. Sensing her behind him, he turned seconds before she shoved the door, almost closing his hand in there.

"What the fuck?"

"Why are you running from me?" she demanded, closing in on him.

"I don't know what you're talking about."

"Yes, you do. Ever since you met Jocelyn, you've been treating me like I'm invisible. What? Did she do something rude?"

"No the ki..." Her eyes darkened, causing him to change what he was about to say. "Jocelyn was fine."

"Then what is it?"

"I don't date women with kids," Chris said bluntly.

"Who asked you to?"

Laughing bitterly, Chris shook his head. "Do you think you're fooling me?"

"So because I don't hide that I find you attractive it means I want to date you?"

"Don't you?" he asked arrogantly.

"You're no Denzel, buddy." Her temper flared, sending off sparks in her deep dark eyes.

"So then, what are you doing here?" he taunted.

"Poker." She gestured around her as if it was obvious.

"Sure you are." Chris smirked, running his gaze up and down her body lecherously.

"Look, Chris, it's true I find you attractive, but just like you don't date women with kids, I don't date men who don't like kids."

"Its not that I don't like them," he denied.

"Then what is it? Before you met Jocelyn, I thought you and I might..." she said, stepping closer.

"Might what?" His voice dropped, deepening in arousal.

Looking at her, Chris could tell she was just as frustrated as he was. Although he knew staying away from her was for the best, he couldn't deny he was tempted. He couldn't chance falling in love with her, because he wouldn't put her or Jocelyn at risk.

"Can we just put all of our cards on the table? You tell me what you want and I'll tell you what I want."

"Fine, you want to know what I want." Chris bent forward until their faces were mere inches apart. "I want to bend you over the counter and fuck you until your knees buckle and your back bends. I want to eat your sweet pussy until the taste of you never leaves my mouth. I want to have you any way and every way I can think of. But then I want to walk away. No weddings, no playing with the kids, no happily ever fucking after. I want to fuck you and leave you. Can you handle that, Eliza?"

"Well, that's not exactly what I want—not that it doesn't sound interesting." Licking her lips, she said seductively, "I want three nights."

"Three nights doing what?"

"Fulfilling three of my deepest fantasies." Running her fingers up his tense arm, Eliza reached the top and scratched him lightly with her nails as she brought her hand back down. "Can you handle that?"

"And then..."

"And then after the three nights, if you want to leave, I'll let you. No tears, no begging, no expectations. You can walk out of my life, and I'll let you." Picking up the cards off the counter top, she handed them to him. "I'll play you for your heart and you can play me for my body."

"Eliza, you won't win."

"Do you want to make a bet?"

Chapter Four

Sitting around the table, Chris realized he didn't need Kayla's bulging breasts or sparkling ring to distract him. Scott flirting with Eliza was distraction enough. The little punk couldn't keep his eyes or his hands off her. He was constantly offering to refill her glass or making some lame joke trying to get her to laugh. But more importantly, he was getting on Chris's last fucking nerve. And to add insult to injury, Eliza was eating it up. You'd think she hadn't been talking about fucking him in the kitchen an hour ago.

Folding his shitty hand, he got up from the table and headed to the kitchen. Grabbing the chips off the top of the fridge, he ripped open the bag, sending potato chips flying.

"Whoa there, Hercules." Dylan entered the kitchen, holding up his hands. "You dirty it, you clean it up."

Scowling, Chris dropped the chips on the counter. Grabbing the broom from the pantry, he swept up the mess. Looking over at the laughing women at the table, he gestured to Scott. "Who's that punk?"

"Who, Scott?" Dylan took a chip out of the bag and munched on it. "He's a college kid who's one of Kayla's test subjects. He's been helping her with her marketing. Seems like an all right kind of guy."

"Test subjects." Frowning, Chris set the broom back. "You mean for the Walnut Wand?"

"Yep, one in the same."

Smiling amusedly, Chris asked. "You mean he used that anal plug on himself?"

"I guess. I didn't ask for any details."

"I didn't know he was gay."

"He isn't."

Snorting, Chris headed back to the table and turned his chair around, crossing his arms at the top. There was no way he was going to let that little bit of information slide. Chris bided his time and waited until everyone had been dealt a new hand. As Scott made yet another un-witty comment, he asked. "So, Scott, did you have any problems fucking yourself with the walnut plug?"

Eliza choked on her drink, her eyes going wild as she struggled to breathe. Chris reached over and patted her on the back as he fought to hold back his grin. Scott's cocky grin faded as Dylan covered his mouth and faked a cough to hide his laughter. Chris knew the Professor would give him hell later, but it was totally worth it to see the smug bastard turn red from embarrassment.

"It's a Walnut Wand," Kayla said, shooting him an evil look from across the table.

Setting down her drink, Eliza glanced over at Scott, who looked like he had just swallowed a football. Turning to Kayla, she asked, "Umm, so is this the wand you were talking about in the park?"

"Yes, it is," Kayla replied defensively. "It's a prostate stimulator I've invented and it's going to revolutionize the sex toy business."

"Yes, it will, honey," Dylan smiled, patting her back. Looking from behind her back, he grinned at Chris, silently urging him on.

"And...umm...you tried it?" Eliza asked, turning towards a fuming Scott.

"Yes, I did."

"Well, that's interesting." She smiled, trying to lighten the mood. "Did you like it?"

"Yes, Skip, tell us all about it," Chris drawled, leaning forward.

"It's Scott," he said angrily. "And it was great. I think Kayla has a real winner on her hands, but I guess someone as close-minded as you wouldn't understand something like that."

"I'm completely open-minded," Chris responded. Looking down at his hand, he paused before adding, "I've just never fucked myself in the ass."

Eliza and Kayla kicked him under the table at the same time, making him jump and rub his shins. "Ouch," he yelped, looking at the glaring women.

"Well, I think it's wonderful, Kayla. I would have never thought of something so inventive. And, Scott, I think it takes real courage to try something like that, to be so free and willing to experiment. Have you tried it, Dylan?" Eliza asked innocently.

"Hell no," he sputtered. Kayla elbowed him, causing him to wince. "Not that I don't think it's a great idea. I'm just a little squeamish when it comes to..."

"Anal toys?"

"No, Kayla's inventions." Holding up his hands to defend himself, he laughed as Kayla hit him again. "Come on, hon, support only goes so far. You're dangerous, but in a good way."

"I am not dangerous," Kayla denied.

Chris had to chuckle at that lie. Kayla was a whiz when it came to computers but put her in front of something as simple as a VCR and she'd have it eating tapes and the TV before the night was over.

"Come on, baby, Scott's lucky you didn't make his intestines explode."

Scott paled at the image and muttered, "Now you tell me?"

Eliza quickly intervened. "I still think it's wonderful. I mean, I don't even own a toy."

Everyone stopped talking and turned their heads to stare at her. Shrugging her shoulders sheepishly, she replied, "I've got a little girl who's very inquisitive."

"Have you ever heard of a lock and key?" questioned a shocked Chris.

"Have you ever heard of manners?" she snapped back.

"I should take you shopping at Harris's," Kayla offered. "My friend Missy works there and she can hook you up with her discount."

"Yeah, that's what she needs, discounted sex toys," joked Dylan. Everyone laughed, breaking the tension in the room.

Looking down at her chips, Eliza said, "Well, I'm getting really low on money here, so I'm thinking this is probably going to be my last hand."

"You could always wager something else," teased Scott.

"Yeah." Looking at him, she raised a finely arched brow. Fingering the gold cross around her neck, she inquired, "What do you have in mind? The only jewelry I'm wearing is this cross and I'm kinda attached to it."

"Well, that's a lovely dress you're wearing," he said, leaning closer to her. "This could quickly turn into a game of strip poker."

"Over your dead body," Chris said firmly to Scott. His chilly tone caused Eliza to turn and look him up and down. Chris knew she was annoyed, but if she thought he was going to let her strip in front of the little punk, she had another think coming.

"And you're going to stop me how?"

"Try me." Turning his cold stare towards her, Chris felt his palm itch. He didn't know what would appease him more, knocking Scott out or paddling Eliza's ass.

"You may be the boss of her at work, Chris, but this is my apartment and if she wants to strip she can," said Kayla, who was still irked with him for his earlier comment about her Wand.

"Yeah, buddy." Dylan smirked, leaning back in his chair with a beer. "If she wants to take if off, I say let her."

"Exactly," Kayla nodded in agreement. "In fact, I might just join her."

Sitting up quickly in his chair, Dylan slammed his bottle on the table and frowned at her. "Do it and you won't sit comfortably for a week."

"Dylan," she gasped.

Holding up her hand to stifle the argument, Eliza rose from the table. "I'll keep my clothes and make this my last hand. Can I use your phone, please?" she asked the feuding couple.

"Sure, use the one in the bedroom," Kayla said as she stared angrily into Dylan's eyes. Standing up as well, Kayla walked into the kitchen with Dylan quickly following behind her.

As Eliza walked away from the table, Chris fumed at the way Scott was staring at her ass. Standing up, he leaned forward and said softly so his voice wouldn't carry to Kayla and Dylan. "Back off, college boy, before I lodge that anal plug so far in your ass, your head will vibrate."

Scott gulped nervously as Chris nodded his head to affirm what he said. Walking after Eliza, he stood outside the bedroom and waited for her to come out. Leaning against the door, he crossed his arms over his chest and guarded the door. Glaring the whole time at Scott, daring him to come near her.

Opening the bedroom door, Eliza rolled her eyes at Chris. "What are you, my bodyguard?"

"Do you need one?"

"The only thing I need protecting from is you, you big bully."

"What did I do?" he demanded.

"Did you have to embarrass that kid?"

"Did you have to encourage him?" he asked in the same mocking tone.

"Do you care?"

Changing the subject, he nodded to the closed door. "Did you really have to make a phone call or were you trying to escape from the argument you started?"

Shocked, she shook her head in amazement. "Your grasp of reality is actually frightening, you know."

"Who did you call?"

"I had to check on Jocelyn."

"The ki... Is she okay?"

"Fast asleep."

"Are you picking her up after you're done?" he questioned nonchalantly.

"No, she's going to stay at my parents." Cocking her head to the side, she asked, "Why do you care? I didn't think you even liked her."

Wincing, he looked down, feeling slightly ashamed. He hadn't given her a reason to think otherwise, but he still wasn't happy she thought that. "She seemed all right. It's not that I don't care or anything."

"Of course not." She shrugged. Looking over his shoulder at Scott, she commented, "Scott looks lonely; maybe I'll go keep him company." When Eliza tried to walk around him, Chris blocked her way and grabbed her arm.

"Lead him on and you'll regret it." His eyes narrowed in anger.

Yanking her arm away from him, Eliza pushed him away from her. "You're starting to piss me off, Chris."

"It's about Goddamn time." Grabbing her, he pulled her in for a punishing kiss. His full lips encased hers. Pushing his tongue into her mouth, he swiped it fluidly against hers, urging her to respond to him.

Eliza reached up, wrapped her arms around his thick neck and pulled him in closer. He devoured her mouth, drinking in her tangy flavor, lemony from her soda. Running his hand around her neck, he went to pull her in even deeper when a cough from behind him reminded Chris where they were. Pulling back, he looked over his shoulder at an amused Dylan.

"Care to finish this hand up?" he asked amusedly.

"We'll be right there," he replied, looking back into Eliza's aroused face. There was no turning back, not after he finally had a taste of her.

"Set your terms," he demanded.

"For what?" she asked confused.

"The way I look at it, the only way I'm going to get you out of my system is to fuck you out, so I agree to your insane deal. What do you want?"

"I told you. Three nights." Eliza pulled away from him. Crossing her arms under her chest, she leaned against the wall. "My way, any way, any time I want you."

"Deal." Leaning forward, he bent down until his face was inches away from hers. "I want you, my way, any way I want you." Looking down at her moist lips, he added, "Or should I say, my way, any hole, any position."

Licking her lips excitedly, she asked, "For how long?"

"Until I say when. Do you accept?"

"Yes." Reaching her hand out, she slid it between his legs and cupped his erect cock through his jeans. "Do you want to shake on it?"

Grabbing her hand, he pushed it firmly into him. "No, this is fine."

Pulling her hand back, she looked over at the table. "Just so we're clear, winner doesn't have to win the entire hand. We just have to beat each other."

"Yes," he said nodding. "I don't want you to try to weasel out."

Snorting she replied, "Don't worry, I won't."

Walking around him, she headed back into the living room and took her place at the table. Kayla was already shuffling the deck, and she seemed as irritated as before. Handing the cards to her right, she asked if Dylan wanted to cut, and he declined.

"Seven card stud, jokers wild," she said as she dealt out the cards.

Dylan groaned mockingly. "Why do we have to play with anything wild? Jokers never work for you anyhow."

"We'll see," she said, frowning at his tone. "Let's do winner takes all. Everyone toss everything into the pot."

Everyone agreed and pushed their chips forward. Kayla went around the table, dealing everyone three cards down. She continued until everyone had four face cards up and three down.

Scott, who had the lowest hand, with only a pair of sevens showing flipped over his last face-down card to reveal nothing. He groaned good-naturedly at his hand. "Who needs college tuition anyway?" he kidded.

Eyeing Eliza over his hand, Chris realized he was in a win-win situation. It didn't matter to him who won or not. Either way, she was going to be his. He had two pairs already showing, the tens and sixes. He flipped his other cards over with ease. His second to last card was the ten of clubs, giving him a full house. Smiling cockily over at Eliza, he imagined all the things he was going to do to her and shifted in his seat to give his hardening cock a little extra room. Since she had a babysitter tonight, there was no reason why they couldn't begin right after the game.

Eliza rolled her eyes at his cocky grin and quickly turned over her first card. She already had three jacks, and when she turned her first card over she immediately realized she had beaten him, as the fourth card was the last jack, the jack of hearts.

Throwing him a mock kiss, she mouthed to him "You're mine" and sat back happily in her chair. Chris didn't feel a moment of disappointment. Her way, his way, it didn't matter to Chris. As long as her fantasy involved him coming inside of her, he was a happy camper.

"Aren't you going to turn over your other cards?" asked Dylan, waiting patiently for his turn.

"No need," she said, never taking her eyes off Chris. He smirked at her smartass answer, feeling his cock jerk in response.

"Same time, honey?" Dylan asked a nervous Kayla when it was his turn.

"Bite me," she muttered, waiting for him to show his hand.

"Oh, I intend to," he teased. From the look of them, Chris wondered if he and Eliza weren't the only ones wagering on the game.

Dylan flipped over his hand, revealing he too had a full house, two queens and three nines.

Kayla groaned and closed her eyes. She already showed a pair of aces, the ace of spades and the ace of clubs, as well as the queen and the ten of spades. Flipping over her cards quickly, Chris laughed at her tightly closed eyes before looking down at her hand.

"Son of a bitch," he and Dylan both muttered at the same time, the only difference was Dylan went extremely pale.

Chris was fucking amazed. The Professor had to be the luckiest person in the world. She had a flush, of the royal variety. She had flipped over the king of spades, a six of diamonds and a joker, her wild card.

Opening her eyes, she let out a wild cry and jumped up from the table. She hopped up and down shouting "yes" as everyone else laughed. Everyone except Dylan, who stared unblinking at her joker. From his ashen face and slack jaw, Chris wondered if Scott wasn't the only one who the Professor would be experimenting on.

Looking over at a smiling Eliza, Chris said loud enough to be heard over Kayla's excited banter, "You and I have a few things we need to discuss, don't you think?"

Nodding her head, she replied, "Oh, yes, yes we do."

Chapter Five

Leaving the card game, Eliza felt exhilarated. The party had broken up soon after the last hand. Although Dylan had desperately wanted them to stay longer, she and Chris made their excuses, both brimming with anticipation. Walking out, Chris pressed the button for the elevator as she and Kayla chatted.

When the elevator arrived, Chris stepped in and waited with his hand holding the doors open as Eliza and Kayla hugged one final time. Scott stepped out of the apartment as Eliza walked into the elevator, and as Scott walked towards them, Chris sent him a chilling glare and let go of the doors. "Can we help you?" raising one eyebrow staring at Scott. Scott scowled as the door shut in his face

"That wasn't very nice," Eliza said, turning towards him frowning.

"So you're surprised I did it. Why?" he asked, walking towards her slowly. Eliza's mouth went dry as he stood over her, staring down into her face. She felt caged in, as if his presence sucked all the air out of the elevator. Chris reached out, releasing the clip in her hair, and ran his fingers through it, bringing it down around her shoulders.

"Stop it," she said, trying to remove his hand from her hair.

"Make me." Pushing her against the elevator wall, Chris dipped his head and captured her mouth with his. His tongue thrust between her parted lips and danced against hers. The elevator came to a stop, halting their kiss. Slipping his hands out of her hair, Chris pulled back and groaned. "You're driving me crazy." He stepped away from her just as the doors opened.

Eliza tried hard to gather herself together. She could feel his heated stare on her as she walked out of the elevator. As they exited the lobby, Chris followed her to her car and told her firmly, "I'll follow you home," daring her to disagree.

"Fine," she said, getting into her car. The ride was over before she was ready. Eliza hadn't been with a man since she and Javier had separated three years ago. She was nervous and apprehensive, and her bravado had all but disappeared as he followed her up the stairs to her apartment.

"Do you want some coffee?" she asked, unlocking her apartment door. Pushing it open, she stepped in to the cool room and held the door as he followed her in. Chris was as silent as a cat, walking in behind her. He watched as if studying her, trying to gauge her next move. His body was taut, his muscles tense beneath his white Old Navy T-shirt.

Chris stepped back as she shut the door, then closing the distance between them, he placed his hand flat against the door. Eliza turned around and looked up at him towering over her. He leaned forward, closed his flat hand and made it into a fist against the door, inches from her face. Turning her head, she pressed a light moist kiss on his forearm. Eliza brushed her soft cheek against his chest and rubbed against him like a kitten.

Growling, Chris unleashed his pent up desire and, bending forward, roughly took her mouth under his. The kiss was all about passion, no finesse, no gentle touches. They kissed deeply and urgently, tongues fighting, lips bruising, both fighting for control. Pulling back from her mouth, he took her bottom lip between his teeth and nipped at it as he slid his fingers between them to work at the buttons of her dress.

Sliding one thin strap off her shoulder, Chris lowered his head and kissed the top of her exposed breasts. She was wearing a strapless bra that pushed her breasts up as if they were begging for his attention. Unable to free them without letting her go, Chris groaned. He reached down, grabbed her thighs and lifted her.

Eliza grabbed him around the neck as he picked her up and spun her away from the door. To her surprise, although she was hardly a lightweight with her full breasts and bountiful backside, Chris carried her across the room as if she weighed nothing.

Walking her backwards, Chris stood between her spread legs, pushing her up high against the opposite wall next to the kitchen bar. Shoving the stool out of his way, he jerked up her dress, exposing her smooth thighs. Chris slid his large callused hands up her skirt, lightly scratching her soft skin in his haste to reach her pussy. Forcing his hand under her sheer lace panties, he began to stroke her with his forefinger. Eliza's pussy was so wet she could hear him stroke against her, pushing between her bare lips, up to the erect bud of her clit.

Moaning, Eliza reached between her open legs and struggled with his belt trying to free his cock from his pants. Chris pushed her hands away. Pulling back, Eliza looked up at him, frustrated.

"I won, Chris. My way, remember?"

"Are you saying this is part of your fantasy?" Pushing his groin against her. "Getting fucked against a wall?"

"No, but..."

"Then it's my way this time," he said, sliding his hand into the top of her bra. Squeezing her nipple, he palmed her full globes. "I've been wanting this for too long."

Scooping her mouth back under his, he kissed her, breaking off as she tried to deepen it. "This time is my time."

Eliza nodded, unable to speak, desire flooding her senses as her arousal flooded her panties. Damp from excitement, she shook as she ran her hand up his taut arm, feeling around his bulging biceps. She knew that as big as he was he could hurt her, but despite his speech, he never would.

Satisfied with her answer, he took her mouth under his and lifted her up from the wall setting her down on the bookcase next to the bar. Pushing the picture frames off the top, he centered her and moved her dress out of his way. Chris broke away from her mouth and placed his lips against her neck, sucking gently for a second before he nibbled up her neck to her ear. "My way, right, Eliza?" he said, ripping away her thong and plunging his finger into her hot cunt.

"Yes," she gasped as his finger worked its way in and out of her moist channel.

He was gently working her open, trying to stretch her so she would be able to accommodate his large member. Chris probed her, carefully adding a second finger, speeding up his rhythm as she ground her pussy down on his hand, soaking him with her juices. Her body began to accept him, stretching around him, receiving his fingers with ease.

With his other hand, Chris reached between them and unbuttoned and unzipped his pants. He pushed them down around his hips along with his underwear, freeing his throbbing erection. Taking his cock in his hand, he ran it against Eliza's wet cunt and tapped it on her clit, chuckling huskily as she whimpered with need.

When Chris slid his wet fingers from her and brought them between his waiting lips, Eliza thought she would just die. The man was sexy as all get out. Releasing her abruptly, Chris grabbed at his pants on his hips, and he reached into his pocket to take out a condom. Ripping into the foil impatiently, he took out the condom and slid it on his cock in one stroke.

Centering his cock at her entrance, Chris eased into her slowly, letting her body adjust to his girth. His thickness stretched her, causing Eliza to cringe slightly.

"Do you want me to stop?" he asked, pulling back slightly.

"Do you want me to kill you?" she said, digging her nails into his shoulders.

Reaching down, he grasped the hem of his shirt and pulled it over his head. Chris slid his hands under her bare bottom and eased her backwards at an angle to deepen his thrust. He pulled back, lifted her and slid into her tight pussy with one steady powerful stroke. His cock, thick and hard, pounded into her.

Eliza gasped loudly as she dug her nails into him, whimpering as Chris sank all the way in her tight pussy. "Don't stop, don't..."

Pulling her down onto him, he grasped her thick hips in his hands and pumped her up and down his cock. Her pussy clenched around him tightly, drawing him in deeper as he fought to pull out. Wrapping her legs tighter around him, she bucked and writhed on him, milking his cock with the tight walls of her cunt.

"Más duro, Chris," she chanted over and over again as he powered into her. Screaming out, she arched and thrust against him, as she came. Leaning forward, she pressed her mouth against his shoulder and bit down hard as she quivered and shook around him.

Groaning, he muttered harshly, "Fuck," and pushed into her harder, throwing back his head he came.

As if sated, Chris dropped his head forward on her breasts. Eliza tried her best to calm her pounding heart, but with him laying on her, it wasn't an easy task. She had never been made love to so intently and so fiercely in her entire life. There was no doubt about it; Chris was well worth the wait.

"Wow," she said as her vagina contracted around his semi-hard cock.

Sucking in his breath, Chris moaned as he arched into her again automatically. With a shaky laugh, he slowly pulled out of her tight sheath.

"You're welcome," he said, lowering her feet to the ground. Looking down at his groin, he grimaced at the mess. "Where's your bathroom?"

"I'll show you, as soon as I can feel my legs." Eliza leaned back against the wall, watching him out of lazy green eyes.

He gave a purely masculine chuckle and pulled her from against the wall. Pulling up his pants, he left them undone with his cock lying loosely through the opening as he followed her down the hall.

Turning on the light, she gestured to the commode and reached in the shower to turn on the water. Lifting her dress over her head, she reached behind her and unclasped her bra.

Chris turned around, buttoning his pants, but paused as she stood completely naked in front of him. "It's a good thing we got that first time out of the way."

"Why?"

"Because now I can take my time and enjoy it." Chris unbuttoned his pants before stepping out of them and pushing back the mauve shower curtain. Stepping under the warm water, he reached out his hand to her and helped her in.

Eliza watched as water fell on him, coating him with a liquid sheen. His body looked like bronze marble, smooth and hard. His chest was very defined and cut like a Greek statue. As if he was carved out of granite. The only difference was Michelangelo never carved a heart tattoo on *David*. Running her fingers over the inked scar that bore the name "Tay" across his chest, she lightly scratched her nails against it and asked, "Who's Tay?"

Moving her away, he seemed a little embarrassed. "My sister," he said, soaping up his chest, covering the fading tattoo.

"Why do you have your sister's name tattooed on you?"

"If I say it's a black thing, will you let it go?"

"No, because that's bullshit."

"Too much alcohol and too much time. Okay?"

"As in jail time?" she asked, shocked. Eliza would have never guessed. Chris always seemed so refined and polished to her.

"Juvie. I did it to remind myself why I had to keep it together." He turned into the spray, shielding his features. His back was stiff, his demeanor shouted "back off". For once Eliza took the hint. Taking her peach scrubby, she poured the peach scented soap onto it and started to scrub his back. Looking over his shoulder, he sniffed the air and frowned.

Turning back around, Chris took the scrubby out of her hand. "No..." he groaned. "Now I'm going to smell like a woman."

"And what's wrong with my soap?"

"Nothing on you," he said, picking up the bottle, squeezing it and pouring the liquid directly on to her full breasts. "But now I feel all sissified. I must do something manly to rectify this."

The liquid slid down between her breasts, down her flat stomach, into her bare lips. Chris reached over and ran the soap with his hands all over her front, lifting her breasts and squeezing her wet slick nipples between his fingers.

"You know what I'd change about that first time?" Looking up from his pinching fingers with arousal in his eyes, he pulled her to him and turned her so her back was to him. Running his hands down her body and up again to cup her breasts. He pushed his stirring cock into the valley of her rear.

"No." Leaning into him, she arched her back, pushing her breasts deeper in his hands.

"I would have paid these beauties some attention." Pulling on her dusky brown nipples, he rubbed the erect tips between his fingers, tugging on them slightly, shooting pleasure straight to her overworked cunt.

"It's not natural to do this more than once a night," she murmured, arching her back. Her body was on fire again, as if they hadn't just spent the last fifteen minutes pounding into each other against the wall.

"You've been with the wrong men, then."

Turning around, she stood on her tiptoes and kissed him. "I could have told you that."

Picking her up, he rubbed her soapy front against his. His cock was once again hard against her stomach, pressing into her. Sliding her hand between them, she soaped his dark member, watching as the dark purplish head disappeared and reappeared in her tan hand. The contrast of the color was startling yet arousing at the same time. He groaned as she tightened her hold on him, stroking his taut cock.

Chris slid his soapy hand down her back between her cheeks washing her intimately, circling her rosette with his finger. Eliza jumped at the personal contact.

Chuckling softly, he asked, "Virgin?"

"Of course."

"We'll see how long that lasts."

"No, Chris," she said, licking his wet nipple. Pulling it between her teeth, she nipped at it, biting down on it gently. "You're too big."

"It'll fit, trust me." Running his hand down her curvy backside, he grabbed her and squeezed gently. Pushing her into him again, he rubbed her middle against his cock, inhaling deeply at the sensation.

Turning in the shower, he placed her under the spray and helped her rinse off. Soaping his hands, he gently massaged her scalp as he washed her hair. Sighing, Eliza enjoyed the sensation of someone else taking care of her for a change. Rinsing her hair out, Eliza looked up at him and saw her desire reflected back in his eyes.

"Bath time over?" she asked huskily.

"Yes," he murmured, bending down and kissing her again.

Eliza had never been made love to so sweetly before. After stepping out of the shower, Chris dried her, even toweling her hair until he got some of the dampness out. Following her into the room, he laid her down on her bed and kissed his way down her body. Stopping briefly to tongue her breasts, he pushed himself between her legs and softly blew cool air against her hot clit. Without spreading her lips, he teasingly licked her outer lips before giving in to her demands to deepen his kiss. He gripped her ass in his hand, pulling her tighter into him as he stabbed his tongue deep into her.

Eliza lay back and let him work his away around her vagina. She had a feeling he had a better idea of what was going down there than she did by the way he brought her twice to orgasm. The second time, she came screaming, pressing his smooth head between her thighs. And when she felt like she could take no more, he entered her again, this time more tender than before. Pushing into her welcoming body, Chris rode her with tenderness and expertise, dragging from her weak body a third and final climax seconds before he came, clamping down his howling mouth on her shoulder, biting down into her flesh.

Waking up slowly, Eliza was amazed she had fallen asleep. The last thing she remembered was coming. Smiling to herself, she opened her eyes and flexed her toes under the cover, stretching her calves. She felt deliciously sore. She ached and tingled in all the right places. Hell in some of the wrong ones too, she thought with a smile and a giggle.

Feeling the bed dip, Eliza looked over her shoulder and saw Chris easing out of the bed. Looking past him to the clock on the nightstand, she grimaced at his attempt to escape.

"You have somewhere to be at four?" she asked, rolling onto her side, facing him.

Chris froze in mid-motion. Turning around, he glanced at her, frowning. "Yeah, I do."

"Where?"

"Home."

Walking out of her room, Chris headed down towards her bathroom as Eliza fumed in bed. There was no way she was going to let him get away with that. If he thought he could just leave and she wasn't going to say anything, he had another thing coming.

Getting out of her bed, Eliza went to the dresser and pulled on her 49ers football jersey. She stepped out of her room just in time to see Chris coming out of her bathroom with his pants on. Moving past her, Chris picked up his shirt off the floor and put it on. Annoyed beyond belief, Eliza walked over to the front door and stood in front of it, blocking his exit.

"Is that all I get?" Eliza inquired as he came to a stop in front of her. His discomfort was obvious as he tensed up. His defensive look quickly melted into a roguish one, the only thing not changed was the scared look in his eyes. Something had messed with him, she could tell, but as usual, he was going to try to hide it behind a cold distant façade.

"I hate to fuck and run."

"As if you could run," she said, crossing her arms across her chest. "You owe me."

"What, five times doesn't count?" Chris replied snidely.

"Remember?" Cocking her head to the side, she said in a mocking tone. "My fantasies don't include getting fucked against a wall."

"Or the shower or the bed?"

"No."

"What do you have in mind then? Give me a half hour and we can try it your way."

"Umm, a half hour, pity. I would have expected more from you, Chris. I guess we'll just have to wait until next time."

"I'm not going to play some fucking little game with you, Eliza."

"Too late, Chris, a deal is a deal." Stepping out from in front of the door, she reminded him, "My way, any way, that was the agreement."

"And this," he said, gesturing around them. "What would you call this?"

"An appetizer."

Chapter Six

The heat and the smell of sweat rushed out the opened door as Dylan entered Wilson's Boxing and Fitness Gym. The Gym was co-owned by Chris and his foster father Eddie Wilson, and it was the one place Dylan knew Chris went when he was upset.

After several unreturned phone calls over the weekend, Dylan had finally called Eddie to ask if he had seen Chris, and lo and behold he had. Looking around the heated room, Dylan easily spotted Chris. Out of all the men there, Chris was the only one pounding the tar out of the punching bag. Sure other men were punching the bag, but Chris was the only one who looked like the bag had robbed him at gunpoint and was taking it out on it. Shirtless, his muscles rippled with each punch he threw.

Walking past Eddie's office doors, Dylan peeked in and nodded to the older man. Black as sin, but sweet as candy, Eddie was the only real father Chris had ever known, and Dylan knew the older man meant the world to Chris. Eddie had been a steady visitor to their dorm room. He even managed to get Dylan in the ring a time or two.

Although Chris was rather closemouthed about his childhood, Dylan knew enough not to pry.

Eddie was on the phone, but he gestured for Dylan to come in. Stepping into the room, he walked over to the bookcase across from the desk and looked at the trophies and family photos prominently displayed on several shelves. Pictures of a younger Chris, sullen and angry, standing next to Eddie, his wife Mildred, and Chris's sister Tay. Looking from the earlier photos to the later ones, Dylan was amazed by the difference in Chris. Not in his face or his body but in his stance. In many ways, he was still like the little boy in the first picture, wary and defiant, but in many ways, he wasn't. Chris didn't get softer; he just got older and less angry.

"How you doing, man?" said Eddie, placing the phone in the cradle. Standing, up he walked around his desk and stuck out his hand, offering it to Dylan.

Smiling, Dylan shook his hand and was engulfed by the larger man in a big bear hug. Although he was pushing his late sixties, Eddie was as strong as many men thirty years his junior. Years of boxing had taken its toll on his features. His wide nose had been broken so many times it had a permanent dent in the middle. A large scar marred his face next to his eyes, and he'd been in dentures a lot sooner than he should have been. But despite his rough features, his face glowed with kindness. His dark brown eyes twinkled and he was seldom without a grin on his wide lips.

"Did you come to go a couple of rounds?" he teased.

"No," chuckled Dylan. "I'm here to check in on Chris."

The smile fell from Eddie's face, and he looked over Dylan's shoulder at his son pounding into the red bag. "Something's going on with him, huh?"

"I don't know. He was at my apartment on Friday, and we were supposed to get together this weekend, but I haven't heard from him."

Nodding, Eddie headed out the door, and he and Dylan walked over to a heavily sweating Chris, who looked like he was seconds away from dropping.

"Enough," Eddie said, and when Chris continued, he walked next to him and bellowed in a voice few dared to cross, "Enough!"

Chris backed off, sweating and breathing hard. He squinted to keep the sweat from dripping in his eyes, and his face was haggard from the strain he had been putting on his body. Shaking a little, he grabbed his water bottle and walked around to prevent stiffening up. The muscles in his chest pulsated from strain, jumping beneath his flesh like salmon trying to get up stream.

Walking over to a bench set against the brick wall, Chris picked up a towel and ran it over his wet skin. His gray shorts, darker in color around his waist from sweat, were riding low on his lean hips. Tired and exhausted, Chris looked at the two men standing in front of him wearing similar frowns.

"What?" he asked, bewildered.

"How long have you been going at it?" Eddie asked, gesturing to the punching bag.

"I don't know, an hour maybe, why?"

"That's too much and you know it," Eddie growled, stepping closer menacingly. "If you want to kill yourself you do it outside my gym."

"I wasn't trying—" he cut off as Eddie scowled deeper. "Sorry, Pop, I wasn't thinking." Eddie might be kind, but he didn't take any shit, even Dylan knew that.

Nodding his head, he turned to go back to his office. Pausing, he stopped and added, "Call your mother. She's got some new little dilly hopper she wants you to put together."

"Yes, sir."

Chris plopped down on the bench and stretched out his legs in front of him. Dylan stood in front of his friend and stared down at him worriedly. Chris looked up at him and frowned. "Yes?"

"What's up?"

"With what?"

"With you, man." Dylan asked, sitting down next to him on the bench. "I kept expecting the Rocky theme to start playing."

"He robbed Apollo of that title."

Dylan rolled his eyes at the old argument. Being roommates with a boxing freak was hell when it came to classic movies like Rocky. "Man, he lost fair and square."

"Look at the tapes," he said, passing the bottle of water to Dylan. "The proof is in the video."

Dylan snorted. "Apollo lost, the only thing Foreman was good at is grilling, and Tyson was the best fighter of all time before he bitched up in jail."

"Ha! Ali is the best fighter of all time, and Tyson can still beat your ass."

"Only if he tripped in the shower picking up the soap."

Chris laughed and looked around the gym at the young men boxing. Turning to him, Dylan watched the play of emotions run across his dark face. It was hard sometimes to read Chris, and normally he would just leave him alone, but something seemed up. Trying to lighten the mood, he asked, "So you and Eliza seemed awfully friendly in the hall on Friday."

"And?"

"And? Is that all you have to say?"

"Yes."

"Come on, give me some details," Dylan goaded.

"Okay," Chris said turning to face him. "After you tell me what bet you lost with the Professor on Friday."

Dylan could feel the color drop from his face. He knew when to call a draw a draw, and besides he never wanted to talk about that night. Not even in the therapy he was going to need soon.

"Changing the subject," Dylan said quickly. "Where were you this weekend? I thought we were going to get together."

"Sorry, man, I had some other stuff come up."

"All weekend, you lucky dog."

"The bet was..."

"You're no fun," he grumbled sitting back against the wall.

"Did you know Eliza had a kid?" Chris asked quietly.

Dylan groaned inside. Although Chris didn't say much about his childhood, Dylan knew Chris had issues with it. Nobody goes to foster care for the hell of it. And for as long as they'd known each other, Chris had never gone out with women with children. It was his thing. Stupid, but every man had a thing. The only problem with it was Dylan could feel the sparks when those two were in the room. It wasn't like her kid was going to go away, so either Chris had to accept it or back off. And knowing Chris like he did, Dylan could already tell it was too late.

"No, I didn't, but does it matter? I know you guys dig each other, can't you just let it go this once?"

"No." he said firmly. "No kids, I'm not going to..."

"To what?"

Looking away, Chris clammed up. "Nothing. It doesn't matter."

Sighing Dylan shook his head. "You want to go grab some dinner?"

"What about the Professor?"

"She's with her test subjects tonight. Research thing. I just couldn't be there." Dylan grimaced.

"What, bringing back too many memories?" teased Chris.

Dylan shot him an evil look, causing Chris to burst out laughing. Jerking his head in the direction of the door, Chris said, "I want a huge burger, and details."

"Burger you can have," he said, standing up. "But as far as the rest of it...over my dead cold body."

"But—"

"Dead cold body."

This weekend totally blew as far as Eliza was concerned. Not only did Chris not call but the bastard didn't even stop by. Not that she had expected things to just be hunky dory after they made love, but the least he could have done was stay the night, the rat bastard.

Pulling back the floral comforter on her bed, Eliza looked down at her rumpled sheets. Jocelyn had a soccer game on Saturday and they had been out all day, and Saturday night she had fallen asleep on the couch. Today was laundry day, and yet she was reluctant to do her sheets.

Flipping up the ivy colored top sheet, she looked over at the left side of the bed that still seemed to embody his imprint in her mattress. Sighing she laid the sheet back down and crawled into bed. Lying on his side, she inhaled his scent that still lingered in the linen. Pulling the sheet over her head, she closed her eyes and tried to transport herself back to Friday. She tried to remember every stroke, every touch, every single moment. But the only thing she could recall was him leaving and the way he did it.

Eliza knew if she were a braver woman, maybe even a stronger woman, she would just say fuck it. But she couldn't because she knew he was worth it, even if he didn't know it.

The opening of her bedroom door pulled her out of her self-imposed funk. Jocelyn came over to the bed and slowly raised the sheet to peek underneath it. Smiling she asked, "Whatcha doing?"

"Taking a nap, do you want to join me?"

"'Kay," she said as she hopped on the bed and slid under the sheet next to Eliza.

Eliza pulled her in close and spooned her from behind. Her soft curly brown hair tickled Eliza's nose as she pulled her in close. The feel of Jocelyn's tiny bones and small frame made Eliza cuddle her more. There was nothing more self-assuring than the feel of her child in her arms. This delicately made angel had once been inside of her, nestled under her heart. It was an image that never failed to bring tears to her eyes. The soft scent of candy and powder drifted up from Jocelyn, mixing in with the faint manly scent of Chris. Inhaling deeply, Eliza fantasized briefly of what it would be like to be surrounded with this scent forever.

"You tired, Momma?" the soft voiced asked.

"No, sweetie, just taking a break."

"You want me to help make the bed?"

"No, Momma needs to take the sheets off so I can wash them." Pulling the sheet from over their head, Eliza smoothed down Jocelyn's hair, brushing it out of her mouth.

Rolling over in the bed, Jocelyn laid her head on the pillow and looked into her mother's eyes. Eliza's melancholy mood instantly lifted, as it usually did when Jocelyn was around her. Smiling, she looked into eyes so similar to her own.

"You know what?" she asked her daughter with a teasing glint in her emerald green eyes.

"No, what?"

"I love you more than all the sand on the beaches in all the world."

"And I love you more than all the stars in the sky," Jocelyn said back, continuing their routine.

"I love you..."

"With all my heart," Jocelyn finished, smiling big.

"That's right, Mami, I do." Leaning over, she kissed Jocelyn on her forehead softly. Life didn't get much better than that.

Monday morning came bright and early, as it always seemed to do, bringing with it its usual bumps and falls. Murphy's Law was in full effect, assuring everything that could go wrong would. On Eliza's list of things to do that weekend, going to the grocery store should have been one of them, but because she decided to skip it, she ran out of peanut butter for Jocelyn's lunch, which put them behind for three minutes until she threw something else together. Hurrying past her dresser, she caught her nylons on a partially open drawer, snagging them in the process, forcing her to change them, which ate up another four minutes.

By the time she dropped Jocelyn off at school, she was already ten minutes behind, thanks to traffic and a run by the *Donut Hut.* So by the time she walked in to the office, she was not only late, but also in a pissy mood. In no mood to deal with Chris, that was for sure. And of course, the first person she would see, she thought grumpily, was him, waiting by her desk.

In a nice crisp blue suit, he looked as tempting as a tray of éclairs. He stood at her desk, drinking a cup of coffee. When he noticed she was in the room, he frowned. "You're late."

"Not too late to get yelled at it looks like," Eliza muttered under her breath.

"What was that?" he asked, raising a brow.

"Sorry."

"Do you think you can possibly work over tonight?"

Fuck, she thought to herself, *today just keeps getting better and better. Maybe if I just close my eyes I can pretend this is all a bad dream.* Closing her eyes, Eliza counted to twenty and slowly opened them.

Unfortunately, Chris was still there, she was still awake, and this day was never going to end.

Chris stared at her bemusedly as she plopped into her chair and sighed loudly. "I guess."

Chuckling, he picked up the donuts off her table and opened the box, groaning when he saw the contents. "There are no powdered ones."

"They were all out," she said, closing her eyes and leaning her head back against the chair.

Snorting unhappily, he put them back on her desk with a thump. "How come I'm the one who always gets screwed out of his donut?"

"No one screwed you out of your donut, there weren't any. It's not a big conspiracy."

"Does this have to do with Friday?"

Slowly opening her eyes, she sent him the most irritated look she could manage. "Yes, Chris, you figured it out. You didn't stay the night so I thought I would punish you by withholding your favorite type of donut," she added sarcastically. "Some women get even by breaking things, I get even by withholding the powder. No cuddling, no powder. Got it?"

Shocked, Chris looked taken aback by her response. Normally Eliza wasn't this bitchy. Not even when that time of the month rolled around. His amazement was almost enough to make her chuckle, almost. Tilting his head to the side, Chris held out his cup to her and said, "Here, I think you need this more than I do." Chris backed away and started down the hall with the unwanted, powderless donuts in hand.

Looking down at the warm black coffee, Eliza brought it up to her mouth and took a sip. Maybe this Murphy's Law wasn't all that bad after all, she thought with a grin.

Chapter Seven

If you had to stay over at work, then sitting across from a beautiful woman, eating Chinese take-out was the only way to do it, Chris thought, scarfing down another bite of his greasy egg roll. It was long past closing time, and they were practically the only ones left there. Mrs. Howard was floating around there somewhere, and a few other stragglers were about, but mainly it was just the two of them.

Sitting back, sighing, Chris rested his hand on his full stomach and watched her from beneath lowered lashes. Like he, she had gotten more comfortable as the night wore on. Her heels were gone and her tiny toes, painted pink, peaked out from the hem of her floral skirt, folded underneath her on the couch.

The print on the skirt reminded him of the hot tropical nights he had spent in Jamaica with some woman whose name he hardly remembered. Chris thought about how much fun he and Eliza would have there, and he could even teach Jocelyn to... Where the hell did that thought come from?

Shaking his head, Chris sat up and glanced over at her again. He had pulled the couch over near the desk, so she would be more comfortable as she went through the files. Yet all it really managed to do was make him imagine what it would be like to have her spread out underneath him on the lush divan. Her long hair spread out above her, her thighs open to receive him. The image went from his head to his cock, instantly causing it to stir.

Eliza hadn't mentioned Friday at all. She hadn't been cold or distant like he'd expected her to be, nor had she been trying to cling to him. She was just sitting there acting as if nothing had even happened, and he wasn't sure how he felt about it.

Clearing his throat to get her attention, he waited until she looked up from what she was doing and said, "I guess I owe you an apology for the way I left on Friday."

Shaking her head, she continued writing. "No, you don't."

Frowning, he wrinkled his brow in irritation. "So you don't want to talk about it?"

"Talk about what? We had a good time, you left, the end. What's there to talk about?"

"Nothing, I guess." Watching her, he wondered if this was an act, or if she really didn't care. Women were hard to read, and no matter how many times he watched Dr. Phil, he was never going to get them. She was just acting so nonchalant he wanted to get a rise out of her, anything to make her as frustrated as he was. "I think you're being pissy."

Glancing up, she frowned at him in confusion. "About what?"

"That I didn't stay and cuddle. Now you're acting funny."

"I'm acting funny? What do you want me to do, climb on your lap and lick your neck? Or pout and whine because you didn't want to stay? I'm a grown woman, Chris. I don't need to act like a needy child. It was fun, hey, maybe we'll even do it again."

"Maybe?" What the fuck, he thought. "What's the 'maybe' shit? What about the bet?"

Putting the folder down, she replied, "What about it?"

"Are you backing out?"

"I hadn't planned on it."

"Then when are we going to start?" Chris hated the way he sounded needy, but he hated the way she was distancing herself more.

"Well, I was giving that some thought."

"And?"

"Well, I want to do something you've never done before."

Roaring with laughter, Chris commented, "Like what?"

"I don't know, what haven't you done?"

"Honey…" Sitting back smiling, he replied cockily, "I've done it all. There's nothing new to me under the sun."

"You seem so jaded.

"I'm not jaded, I've…let's just say…a few more experiences than you have."

Snorting, she placed her feet down on the ground. "Well, I would hope so. I've been with three men, if you include yourself."

That completely amazed him. He knew she felt tight, but the fact a beautiful, attractive woman had only slept with two men before him was mind numbing. "Only?" he questioned.

"Yes." Smirking, she asked, "Why, how many women have you slept with?"

How many people have you slept with was not his favorite game to play. You could never tell with women what was the right thing to say. And where he was happy she hadn't slept around, it was really a good thing he had. Everything he learned she would benefit from, not that she would see it that way though.

"Numbers aren't important," Chris said, trying to avoid the question.

Brows drawing together in a frown, Eliza stiffened up at his remark. "If I said that, you would be flipping out."

"No, I wouldn't," he remarked defensively. "We're fucking. This isn't a relationship." That was completely the wrong thing to say. Chris knew it the second it came out of his mouth. Eliza's eyes widened, and her mouth tightened around the corners.

"You wouldn't know a relationship if it bit you in the ass," she grumbled.

"Trust me, if something bites me in the ass, I'm going to know what it is."

"Just tell me."

"Why?"

"Because I want to know," Eliza stubbornly demanded.

"Eliza, this is pointless."

Eliza stood, walked over to his desk and leaned against it, facing him. Arms crossing her chest, she looked determined and single-minded. "Is it more than ten?"

Rolling his eyes, Chris refused to give in. He wasn't going to tell her, no matter how cute she looked. She was in a huff, and her cheeks were flushed with irritation. It was adorable. Even the way her eyes flared like emerald daggers amused him. She was downright indignant.

"More than fifteen?" she insisted.

"I'm not saying." Chuckling, Chris was beginning to enjoy himself.

"If you've had sex with more than fifteen people, that's just gross."

"Prude."

"I'm not a prude, but that's not normal."

"I haven't slept with more than fifteen women," he said, caving a bit. Having her annoyed was okay, but worried and disgusted was another. Chris had slept with his share of women, but he had always been careful. Never once having sex without a condom, and he was annually tested for viruses. "But let's just say there's not much I haven't tried."

"Really?"

"Really."

"Have you ever performed anal sex?" Eliza inquired, tilting her head.

"Yes."

"Sex outside."

"Yes."

"A threesome?"

"Yes."

Her eyebrows rose in shock at his answer. Chris didn't know if this was a bad thing or a good thing.

"You're lying," she voiced in awe.

Laughing, he shook his head and watched her try to get herself back together. He couldn't tell if she was aroused or just amazed.

"Two girls?"

"Once or twice." He smiled.

"With a guy?"

"Once or twice," Chris stated, a bit more uncomfortable with this part. Not the fact he had shared a woman with another guy, but just who the other guy was.

He and Dylan had done a lot of crazy things in college. Women had always been drawn to them. And they had never had any problem getting girls to agree to do anything they asked. But he wasn't so sure how much Dylan had confided in Kayla, and he wasn't about to say anything to mess that up for his friend.

"Did you and he..." Eliza asked, gesturing with her hand.

Chris gave her a look that would have frozen ice cubes. That was not the impression he thought she was going to get. He didn't go that way, not that there was anything wrong with men who did, he just wasn't one of them.

"Sorry." She chuckled.

Putting her hands down to her sides, she ran her fingers lightly back and forth on the smooth curved edge of his desk. She looked kind of upset, and Chris wondered what she was thinking. He didn't have to wonder long.

"I guess you've done a lot," she remarked in a soft tone.

"Yes." Trying to read her expression, he watched her face. "I guess."

Looking down, she turned her face away and Chris finally caught on to what was going on with her. She wanted them to do something special, something he'd never done before, so she could stand out to him. The funny thing was she already did stand out to him. The short time they had spent together on Friday had meant more to him than any of the other women he'd been with before.

Easing his chair forward, he captured her between his legs and pressed her back against the desk. Running his hands up her thighs, he placed them on her hips and looked up at her. "I've never had sex in an office."

Eyeing him carefully, she ran her hands up his arms and back down again, stopping to grip his wrist. "I thought we were discussing my fantasies." Her voice thickened with desire.

"We were," he said, bunching the material at her waist and easing up her skirt. The floral material gathered up her thighs as he inched it up slowly to heighten his senses. "But I too have been giving this some thought and I think we need to renegotiate our bet."

"Really?" she asked softly, her voice catching as he slid his hands underneath her skirt and cupped her bare buttocks. Rocking back in surprise, he ran his hand up her crease and felt the thong string with his fingers.

"Yes," he said huskily. "I think for everything we do for you, we should do something I want to do."

"But that wasn't the deal."

"This is a new deal, a new and improved deal."

"So would Friday count as your turn?"

"No, Friday was as you described it," he said, hooking his fingers on the side of her thong and sliding it down her hips. "An appetizer."

"And this is what, your turn?" she said, placing her hand on his shoulder to steady herself as she lifted up first one foot and then the other to help him ease off her underwear.

"Unless you want to count it as yours." Picking her up, he placed her on the desk bare bottomed and pushed her skirt up over her hips. Spreading her legs, he stared at the glistening lips of her bare cunt and licked his lips in anticipation.

"I don't think so." Leaning back on the desk, she braced herself up on her arms and watched as he moved in slowly to touch her.

Rubbing his fingers against her smooth mound, he asked hoarsely, "How long does it take to get this done?"

Pushing up a bit, she ran her hand over his equally smooth scalp and replied, "How long does it take to do this?"

"I have someone do it for me," Chris said, easing his finger into her moist opening.

Arching her back, she groaned as he filled her with his finger and replied, "So do I."

Pausing in his downward descent, he looked up at her from between her thighs and said, "Maybe we can trade one time, I'll do you and you do me."

Dipping his mouth down, he opened up her lips with his free hand and tasted her. Still fingering her hot tunnel, Chris darted his tongue over her clit and licked in rapid succession before taking the heated bud between his lips and pulling softly. Adding a second finger inside her, he widened her entrance, preparing her for his hard cock. He remembered how tight she was on Friday, and he couldn't wait to plunge back into her taut cunt.

He continued to eat her, drinking her spicy essence like it was the water of life. Speeding up his plunging fingers, Chris worked her as she quivered around him. Her thighs shook, and she laid back, freeing her hands to pull his face closer in, squeezing her legs together as she came, screaming something he didn't understand.

Pulling up, he wiped his mouth with his shirtsleeve and reached in the back of his wallet and pulled out a condom. Looking down at her trembling body, he released his throbbing erection and sheathed it with the latex.

Pulling her hips closer to him, he positioned her so her ass was at the edge of the desk, partially hanging off. Rubbing his cock around her moist pussy, he teased her as she arched up against him, her opening gravitating towards his hard cock. "*Por favor,* Chris," she begged, pushing up to him. "*Te necesito.*"

Chris placed the head of his throbbing cock at her core and pushed into her pussy slowly, gently taking her, so as not to hurt her. Gritting his teeth, he held himself back from plunging into her as hard and as fast as he wanted to. He wanted to grind into her and ride her until she came screaming his name, but for her sake he didn't.

Biting back an oath, he pulled out slowly and plunged forward carefully. Eliza's body opened, accepting him with greater ease. Putting his hands back on her hips, he began to pick up his speed as he thrust into her welcoming body.

Eliza cried out in pleasure as he thrust into her. Speaking rapidly in Spanish, she arched and moved under him, her body flooding him with her sweet essence. Gripping her tighter, he raised her hips, allowing him to dive deeper inside her. The motion of their fucking caused the desk to shake as he pounded into her.

"*Sí, Papi, más duro,*" Eliza groaned.

Tightening her inner muscles around him, Eliza arched and groaned as she came. She drew him deeper into her, jerking around him as he pulled out once more, before slamming into her and coming.

Leaning forward, he lay against her, panting from exhaustion. His body shook and his cock jerked inside her. When he was finally able to move, he slipped out of her and eased back to sit in his chair. His condom-coated cock lay limp against his pants, a sign of its true tired state.

The air around them, thick and sweetened by their aroma, clung to their damp skin. Eliza eased up, closing her legs and lowering her skirt. Slipping off the desk, she made her way over to the couch cattycorner to his chair and dropped down, limp and sated.

"You know what?" she said, leaning her head back against his couch and closing her eyes. "You are unbelievable."

"You're not so bad yourself."

"By the time we're done with this bet, I'm going to be a candidate for a nursing home," she teased, looking over at him.

Instead of being amused, Chris felt insulted. She spoke as if this was just a fly by night for them, like she wouldn't have a problem easing on to the next man. "Just for the record, sugar," he drawled, "it won't be this good with the next man."

"Oh what, you hold the patent on good sex?"

"Good sex, no, great sex, yes," he replied, reaching over and opening his bottom drawer. Extracting a tissue, he took off the soiled condom, and wiped his limp cock. "But it's a combination of the right elements, and the right people. This won't work just with anyone."

"So does this mean it won't be as good for you with someone else?" Eliza asked, sitting up.

Feeling flustered by what he'd just admitted, Chris answered hesitantly, "Umm, well, I guess."

"Hmm," was all she said as she began to gather up the folders and papers on the couch. Chris watched silently as she straightened up their things. Walking in front of the desk, she picked up the papers that had been thrown aside in their haste to copulate.

"It's getting late," she said, standing in front of him. "I still have to pick up Jocelyn and head home."

"Well, I'll walk you out." Getting up from the chair, he tossed the balled up tissues in the trash. "Just let me go stop at the restroom first."

"It's okay," she said, walking to the closed door,

Lifting up the scrap of panties he had taken off her, he asked, "You might need these."

Blushing, she walked over and reached for them.

Yanking them out of her reach, Chris stuffed them in his pocket and said, "Wait for me and I'll return them."

Eliza nodded stiffly.

Satisfied she would stay and wait for him, Chris opened the door and exited the office. Walking into the bathroom down the hall, he cleaned himself up as much as possible. Heading back to his office, he paused outside next to her desk and noticed her things were gone. Cursing under his breath, he opened his door and stormed inside. Just as he suspected, she had left.

Clenching her panties in his fist, he walked to his desk and noticed a note sitting on top of his keyboard. Leaning over and picking it up, he recognized her handwriting and read it.

Chris,

I think it's fair to say it's my turn. So for fantasy number one you have to make a stop at the adult toy store of your choice. I'm sure with your vast sexual history you'll be able to find one to your liking. Please pick up the following items:

1) Sexual toy of your choice, but please be sure it is safe to use in the water.

2) Vanilla bubble bath and silk bubble beads.

3) Scented candle, vanilla would be great, but feel free to pick something else.

4) Lotion, something you like the scent of.

And last but not least:

5) Chocolate kisses, since we didn't kiss once tonight, I want some kisses I can depend on.

You can deliver these items to my home on Friday night, at seven sharp. Come dressed casually and ready for a night you will never forget.

Eliza

P.S. You can keep the panties as a souvenir.

Chris smiled down at the note in his hand as he caressed the panties in his pocket. He was hoping it would turn out to be a night neither one of them would forget.

Chapter Eight

"Hey, man."

Chris looked up from the phonebook he had opened on his desk to see Dylan standing in the doorway. Smiling good-naturedly, Dylan strolled into the office and sat down in the chair facing Chris's desk.

"What's on your agenda for this weekend?" Dylan asked.

Looking past Dylan into the outer office, Chris said quietly, "I kind of have a date tonight."

"Kind of a date?" Dylan smirked. "What's that mean?"

"It means what I said. A date of sorts."

"With who?"

"No one you know."

"I might, you don't know."

"What's with the fifty questions?" Chris's irritation was beginning to show. He wasn't sure if he wanted Dylan to know about what he and Eliza were doing. Chris knew Dylan would never let him hear the end of it, mainly because if the situations were reversed, he would be teasing Dylan unmercifully.

"Just trying to keep tabs on you. You've been a very busy man lately."

"What, are you feeling lonely?"

"Nah, just nosy."

Reaching over on the desk, Dylan swiped the phonebook from under Chris's hand and read the page he was looking at.

"Gimme that back," Chris muttered embarrassedly.

Looking down at the page Chris had marked, Dylan burst out laughing at the businesses Chris had circled. They were names of adult bookstores, all of them.

Chris leaned over the desk, and snatched the book out of Dylan's hands. He stood, walked quickly to the door and shut it behind him so no one would see him murdering Dylan.

Dylan stood and leaned against his desk with a huge smile plastered across his face. "Now this is a first."

"Shut up."

"If the guys in the dorm could see you now," Dylan teased. "King Dingaling underlining sex stores in his phone book. There's got to be a story here, and I'm not leaving until I hear it."

"Oh, you'll leave all right," Chris hissed. "It's only a matter of whether it will be head first or feet first."

"Come on, you know this is good. If it was me, you'd be crowing."

"Well, it isn't you, it's me,"

"What are you looking for?"

"What do you think, Einstein?"

"You don't want to know what I'm thinking," he joked. "After living with Kayla, I'm pretty much at the point where nothing shocks me anymore."

"Really," Chris drawled. Walking back around the desk, he sat back down in his chair.

"Yeah, I love her, but the girl has got some serious issues." Toying with his tie jokingly, Dylan stretched it out in front of him and stroked it obscenely while wiggling his eyebrows. "Nothing I can't handle, I assure you."

"You want to know what I'm doing?"

"Yes."

"Fine, I'm looking for waterproof sex toys for Eliza and me to use tonight."

Dylan's mouth fell open and he dropped his tie in shock. Chris chuckled at the sight of his cool as a cucumber friend at a loss for words.

"Are you joking?" he asked, his voice lowering.

"Nope."

"Well, hell, I see a lot has changed since the other night."

"Changed enough, that's for sure," Chris agreed.

"If you're serious about this, you know there's only one way to go about it."

"Really, and what's that?"

"Why don't you ask Kayla to go with you?"

"I'm not taking your fiancée with me to a porn store," Chris gasped.

"Why not?"

"Because, man, that's just wrong."

"Ah come on, she'll get a kick out of it."

"No."

"I'll call her right now."

"No."

"These days she's become a porn store expert. She even has her favorite one." Dylan picked up the phone, trying to turn it around, but Chris snatched it out of his hand.

"There's no way in hell I'm going to a dirty store with Rainbow Bright."

"But Chris..."

"When hell freezes over," Chris denied adamantly.

Walking into the store with Kayla, Chris wondered how many lost souls were kicking it up in hell, enjoying the snowstorm, thanks to him. Still amazed he had let Dylan talk him into this, he couldn't believe he was spending his lunch break looking at waterproof vibrators.

Kayla seemed to be in her element though, he had to admit, which only made him curious and worried over his friend's sex life. Shuffling through vibrators, she read aloud the instructions on the back as if it were recipes in a cookbook. To say he was uncomfortable was putting it lightly. It was bad enough he was in a porn store in the middle of the day, but the fact that he was in a porn store with *Kayla* in the middle of the day was almost more than he could bear.

It wasn't hard to see what Dylan saw in her. Kayla was lively and a lot of fun to be with, but Chris wasn't too sure if she was all there. Starting with the fact she always looked like she dressed in the dark. She actually took out a notebook filled with names of sex toys with little stars rating them on the side. And if that didn't beat all, she was actually on a first name basis with the employees.

"Are you finding everything okay?" asked a pretty girl from behind them. Kayla looked over his shoulder and smiled at the employee.

"Chris, this is my friend Missy," Kayla said introducing them. "She works here, and anything you need to know about toys, she can tell you."

Blushing slightly, the plump girl smiled warmly at him. Her soft smile lit up her entire face, giving her a pleasant glow. Fidgeting under his stare, Missy pushed a strand of her chestnut brown hair behind her ear, as she asked, "Was there something in particular you were looking for?"

Flushing faintly, Chris leaned forward and said softly, "Something that can be used in water."

"In water," Kayla muttered, looking down at her notes. "Shit, I didn't even consider that."

Rolling her eyes, Missy smiled as Kayla wandered off notebook in hand to the plugs on the wall. "She'll be there for hours," she warned Chris teasingly. "So this is the best time for us to sneak away."

"This is a little disconcerting," Chris said, following Missy throughout the aisle.

"Why?" she asked curiously.

"I'm not the type who normally would come to a place like this."

"You'd be surprised by all the normal types who come here everyday."

"Oh, I know," Chris backpedaled. "I'm not saying anything is wrong with coming here. It's just..."

"Trust me." Missy smiled. "I understand. So was there anything in particular you were looking for, besides waterproof? Something for both of you, or something geared more to her pleasure?"

"Uhh, maybe a little of both."

Missy pointed out several gadgets and explained to Chris in very non-descriptive terms how they worked. Chris was amazed at how comfortable he felt with her, especially considering their surroundings.

Picking up an item, Chris examined it and asked, "Have you tried this?"

"No."

"What about this one?" he asked, pointing to another.

"No." This time Missy's complexion darkened slightly. "I haven't tried any of these."

"Well, how do you know how they work?"

"You don't have to fall to understand the law of gravity."

"True, but it would help," he replied frustratingly.

"Hey, you guys," Kayla yelled from across the store. "What do you think about me making the wand in different flavors?"

"Is she for real?" Chris asked a bemused Missy.

"I think so."

Shaking his head, Chris took the items they had selected and brought them to the front of the store. He couldn't wait to try them out on Eliza. Just the thought of watching her masturbate with it, or him pleasuring her with it was enough to get his juices stirring. He could still hear the faint sounds of her chanting in his ear. Tonight was going to be a night they would never forget.

Chris left the store without Kayla. Thankful again that they had taken separate cars, he headed back to work. Leaving the bag in the trunk of the car, Chris entered the building and headed for Dylan's office. Nodding to Mrs. Howard, he knocked lightly on the door and waited for Dylan's okay before entering.

Setting the phone back in the cradle, Dylan smiled when Chris walked in. "So did you buy anything good?"

"Several things, yes," he said, shutting the door behind him.

"Like..."

"Nothing I'm going to share," Chris teased, sitting down. "But I will say this."

"Yes."

"Your girl has some serious issues."

Laughing, Dylan nodded his agreement. "Who are you telling, man? I live with her."

"Do you know she was actually sniffing butt plugs?"

Grimacing, Dylan brought his head down to the desk and banged it against it several times. "I really wish you would have kept that to yourself."

Chuckling, Chris replied, "Hey, if I had to shop with her, you had to hear about it."

"Why the hell was she..." Shaking his head, Dylan shuddered. "Never mind. I don't want to know."

Chris laughed at the expression on Dylan's face. Standing, he walked to the door and said over his shoulder, "She also mentioned trying out a new design."

"Arrggg."

Closing the door on Dylan's cry of despair, Chris strolled to his office. Nodding to Eliza, who was typing on the computer, he walked into his office. Tonight couldn't come quick enough for him.

Chapter Nine

Today had come quicker than Eliza had thought possible. Since their night together on Monday, neither one of them had said anything about what happened. She knew he got her note, but he never made mention of it. Not once. That was so not like him.

Tonight was the night. Everything hopefully would go as planned. She wondered what kind of toys he would bring. Knowing Chris it would be something wild.

"Hi, I have a packet for you to sign for," said a deep voice, breaking into her reverie.

Looking up she smiled at the handsome UPS guy. Taking the board, she filled out the appropriate form while chatting with him. Laughing softly at something he said, Eliza flirted lightly with him. She never understood the women who were cold and vicious to men. It was always a compliment when anyone showed you attention, and Eliza, never one to hurt anyone's feelings, always made it point of smiling and chatting back before letting them know she was unavailable.

Taking the form from her, he glanced down at her name and looked back at her. "Eliza, that's a pretty name."

"Thanks." Eliza smiled.

"Is it short for something?"

"It's short for Mrs. Rivera," said Chris coldly from behind her.

Eliza's smile froze on her face as she tried to counter his icy comment with a smile.

"Sorry," the man said, looking up into Chris's stony stare. Backing away quickly, he left as quietly as he had appeared.

Picking up the package off her desk, she turned and thrust it at him, frowning. "Was that necessary?"

"What?" Chris asked.

"That rude comment, and for your information, I haven't been Mrs. Rivera in several years."

"Lower your voice," he demanded looking around the open office. "Come into my office now."

"Arf," she barked. Frowning down at her, Chris narrowed his eyes and waited until she got up and went into his office.

Clenching her fists at her sides, Eliza walked into his office with her head held high. How dare he treat her that way? Her temper, like her passion, was quick to rise in any given circumstances, and today Chris had ignited the wrong one. Spinning quickly around when the door shut behind him, Eliza stormed up to him and poked her finger in his face.

"What is your damage?" she demand

Grabbing her wrist, Chris spun around until her back was against the door. When Eliza raised her other hand to slap him, he caught it and raised them both over her head. Lowering his face until it was inches from hers, Chris said heatedly. "Until this little bet thing of ours is done, I don't want to even see you smiling at another man. Do you understand me?"

"I understand you're a fucking *pendejo*," she spat.

"If I'm crazy, it's because you make me that way." Capturing her angry mouth with his, Chris kissed her until she couldn't breath. Forcing his tongue between her lips, he dominated her mouth, like he wanted to dominate her soul.

Just as Eliza was getting into the kiss, Chris ended it, panting and cursing under his breath. Eliza saw the surprised look in his eyes before he quickly masked it, as if he too was shocked by what he had done. Pulling back, he lowered her hands and jerked in surprise when Eliza grabbed him by his lapel and spun him around until his back was on the wall.

"Understand this, the next time you pull that crap on me I will take you down. You might be bigger and stronger than I am, but I'm an only girl with three older brothers. I know how to fight dirty."

Putting her hands behind his head, she pulled his shocked face down and ran her tongue over his bottom lip before sucking it into her mouth. Biting on it gently, she drove her tongue in his mouth when he let out a gasp. Chris quickly took command of the kiss as he stroked his tongue over hers.

Lowering his hands, he ran them across her bottom and pulled her in closer to him. Lifting her a little, he rubbed her front over his rapidly hardening penis. Eliza took her hands down from his head and wrapped them around his neck. Their kiss deepened as his door was opened. Breaking apart from their kiss, they turned and saw Dylan's head poking around the frame. His eyes opened wide in amazement, followed quickly by a smarmy grin.

Backing away from Chris, Eliza ran her hands down her butter yellow skirt to smooth it back in place.

"Excuse me, I didn't mean to interrupt anything," Dylan teased, coming into the office all the way.

"You didn't," Eliza denied, looking over at Chris, who was still staring at her hungrily. She ran her tongue over her swollen mouth. Chris's gaze followed the path her tongue made, causing her heart to speed up.

Looking away, she walked past Dylan, who was smiling like a Cheshire cat, and opened the door.

"Eliza," Chris called, walking over to her.

She paused, not turning around and waited for his response.

"Seven sharp."

Blushing at Dylan's all too masculine chuckle, she nodded her head and walked out of his office.

♦ ♥ ♣ ♠

Eliza glanced at the clock on her cable box, for what had to be the hundredth time. It didn't make the time go by any faster, nor did it calm her racing heart. It only proved to her in so many ways what a coward she was.

Tugging on her robe more securely, she tapped her foot on the floor to the seconds on the clock. It wasn't even seven o'clock yet, but her nerves were completely shot. Eliza stood and made her way over to the phone, just as her doorbell rang. Pulling tightly again on the belt of her robe, she made her way over to the door and peeked out of the peek hole.

Chris stood in the distorted view with flowers in his hands. Closing her eyes, she said a silent prayer for courage and unlocked the door. Taking in a deep breath, she pulled the door open and smiled up at him.

In black slacks and a maroon long sleeve sweater, Chris looked delicious. The color of the sweater highlighted the red tones in his skin she never knew existed, and the fit of the pants emphasized his powerful legs.

His cocky stance and too sure smile told Eliza that, despite what her fantasy was, he was planning on being in control the whole time, or at least that's what he thought.

"Hello," he said as he handed her the white lilies.

Taking them, she brought them in close and inhaled their floral scent. Looking up from the midst of the flowers, Eliza smiled and said, "This wasn't on the list."

"I know, I improvised, but don't worry," he said, holding up a discreet brown bag. "I picked up the items on your list as well."

"Ooh, Mommy, he brought you flowers," Jocelyn said, peeking around Eliza's thighs. Chris's smile froze as he looked down at the little girl smiling up from behind Eliza. He quickly yanked the bag from in front of him and hid it behind his back.

"Hey, Mr. Chris."

"Hey," he remarked back, looking up Eliza questionably.

"Let's go inside before the neighbors poke their heads out," she said all too cheerfully. Stepping back, Eliza took Jocelyn's hand and pulled her out of Chris's way as he came into the apartment.

His large frame seemed to dwarf her apartment, something she hadn't noticed before. Not that she had had much time to take that kind of thing in before they had gotten hot and heavy. Jocelyn bounced all around her, like a frisky little puppy, excited they had a visitor. When Eliza had told her Chris was coming over to babysit her, Jocelyn had dragged all of her board games into the living room and went through their DVDs, picking out the perfect one for them watch. Judging by Chris's uncomfortable expression, Jocelyn was the only one excited by the arrangements.

"Mami, go get the movie ready. Mr. Chris and I are going to go fix the popcorn."

"'Kay." Letting go of Eliza's hand, Jocelyn ran around the couch and plopped down in front of the entertainment center.

Eliza headed into her kitchen, with a confused Chris in tow. Opening a cabinet on top of her stove, she stood on her tiptoes and reached for a heart-shaped vase in the back. "Here," Chris spoke from behind her, "I'll get it."

Moving out of his way, Eliza went to the sink and turned on the faucet. Handing her the vase, Chris asked, confused, "What's wrong, did your babysitter cancel at the last moment?"

"Not really," Eliza remarked, filling the vase. Setting the full vase on the counter, she unwrapped her flowers as he spoke.

"Running late?"

"No, right on time, as a matter of fact."

"Apparently I'm not getting it. Who's going to watch Jocelyn?"

Turning towards him, she answered, "You are."

"I don't think so."

"I thought this was about my fantasy." Crossing her arms, Eliza prepared to give her little speech she had rehearsed. She knew Chris would have a coronary when he realized what he was really here for, but Eliza didn't care, a deal was a deal.

"Than maybe you ought to explain what your fantasy is."

"Probably the same fantasy as many single working moms, to take a nice long bubble bath, without being interrupted."

"And, where do I come in here?" he demanded.

"Well you're here to ensure I don't get interrupted."

"Well, silly me, here I was thinking sex would have something to do with your little fantasy."

"It does," she said, reaching for the brown bag he had placed on the counter. "That's where these bad boys come in handy."

"You could have had one of your many brothers watch her for you."

"Like I was really going to ask one of my brothers to go buy me some toys. You're the one who was bragging about all of your experience. I knew you'd be perfect for this job."

"I'm not going for this," Chris turned to head out of the kitchen, but Eliza grabbed his arm, stopping him.

"Coward."

Chris stopped tugging on his arm and looked down at her. "What?"

"You heard me," she fumed. "Not everything is about you, Chris. This was about my fantasies, and if you had won, I would have done anything you wanted. Well, this is what I want. So if you break our deal, it's all over, because no matter how great in bed you are, I'll know underneath all this muscle and brawn is a selfish coward who thinks of no one but himself."

The anger and uncertainty radiated off Chris like steam off snow. His tightly clasped jaw creaked under the pressure he was imposing as he bit down. Shaking his head, he walked past her back into the kitchen and muttered "fuck" under his breath.

Eliza waited, wondering what was going on in his head. She knew she was hitting beneath the belt with this one, but she really didn't think she had much choice. She was a package deal, and unless Chris got over whatever his thing was with kids, they would never have a future. Eliza needed to know if he was willing to take a chance. If not, then there was no reason for this to ever go any further.

Jocelyn ran into the kitchen, grinning broadly. "Are you ready, Mr. Chris?" she asked excitedly.

At his silence, Eliza figured he had made his choice. "Mr. Chris has to..."

"Show your momma how a couple things work that I bought her, so give us a minute and I'll be in there," he said, turning around. His smile was forced, but to a little girl hungry for male attention, it was a welcoming beacon.

"Okay." Jocelyn dashed out of the room with an excited shriek.

The smile immediately dropped from his face. "This was low, Eliza."

"You never specified they had to be sexual fantasies."

"How do you know you can trust me with her? How do you know I'm not a pervert?" he demanded.

"Would a pervert care?" she countered. These were all good questions, questions she, as a mother of a little girl, had asked herself countless times before about other men, but never about Chris. How did she know she could trust him? The same way she knew the sun would rise. There were just some things you never had to doubt.

"I've been locked up."

"Where you got a tattoo of your sister's name on your chest."

Chris flushed a little at her comment before shaking his head in denial. Eliza could tell it was taking everything out of him not to just walk out. And the fact he stayed spoke volumes to her.

"Chris, if you're that uncomfortable with it, just leave."

"But if I do, then you and I..." he gestured between them.

"There will be no you and I," Eliza replied softly.

Fuming, he walked in front of her and snatched the bag out of her hands. Reaching inside, he took out the Hershey kisses and slammed them on the counter. Taking out a boxed item, he opened it up and turned it towards her. It was clear and oval with ribs. Looking over her shoulder, to check to see if it was clear, Chris said softly, "This is the Aqua Orb. It's a vibrating egg that's waterproof; you can use it on your nipples or clit."

Reaching in the bag, he pulled out another gadget. It looked like a regular pink bath scrunchy. "This is called the Body Glow, it has a vibrating egg inside."

Piling it on the counter next to the chocolate, he took out her vanilla scented bubble bath, beads and lotion. Reaching in, he pulled out the last item. It was light purple, also see-through, shaped like a small portable phone with a hole in the middle. The top had two things sticking up like little ears, and the opposite end had a little tail-like thing the size of his thumb.

"This is called the Deluxe Beaver. I'm supposed to wear it, so I guess it can stay in the bag, and I can take it back tomorrow," he replied dryly.

Taking it from his hand, Eliza stopped him from putting it back in the bag. "I said not tonight, not never."

"Tonight is yours but don't forget my turn is next."

Picking up the candy, Chris left the kitchen and headed towards the living room, leaving a dazed Eliza staring after him.

Chapter Ten

Grasping the bag of Kisses in his hand, Chris headed into the living room. If he was going to have to watch her kid then he was at least eating the chocolate. Eliza couldn't have the orgasm, the solitude and the candy. That just wasn't going to happen.

The creaking floor alerted Jocelyn to his presence. Spinning around, she saw him and grinned broadly. Hopping up on the couch, she knelt on the cushions, bouncing up and down.

"You ready, Mr. Chris?"

"I don't know," he commented apprehensively. "For what?"

"For the movie and to play cards."

"I don't suppose you know how to play poker," he joked, coming around the couch and sitting as far away from her as possible. Walking over to him on her knees, she reached over on the coffee table and picked up the cartoon-covered cards.

"No, I don't know how to play poker, but I can play Slap Jack, Old Maid and Go Fish."

"Ummm, all that?"

"Yep, my mom says I'm a real card sharp."

"Card *sharp*, huh?" Chris said, biting back a chuckle. "Well, I guess I'll have to be careful around you."

"Yep. I gots a couple of movies in the DVD player, which one do you want to watch?"

"What are my choices?"

Counting off the list on her fingers, Jocelyn tilted her head and said. "*Cinderella, Lion King,* and *Finding Nemo.*"

"You can decide."

"'Kay, we'll watch *Nemo,* it's my favorite." Pointing the remote at the screen, she pushed play and got down on the floor in front of the table. Shuffling the deck, she looked over her shoulder at Chris and frowned. "You have to sit around the table."

"Oh, my bad," Chris remarked getting off the couch. Sitting cattycorner from her across the table, Chris felt like a geek. Here he was, this big man, sitting next to this small little girl, at a smaller table, playing with a deck of Sponge Bob Square Pants playing cards. If the guys at the gym could see him, he would never make it out of the ring in one piece.

Jocelyn shuffled the cards, staring intently at them. She had her tongue poking out of the side of her mouth in concentration. It was actually kind of cute, thought Chris with a slight smile. And the whole time she was doing this, she was talking. He wasn't even sure what she was talking about now, it had started with a sore on her leg and God only knew what it was now.

Dealing the cards one at a time, she slowly placed them down in front of him while she counted out loud. Looking up, she asked, "Do you have seven of 'em?"

Glancing down, he counted and said yes.

"Good, do you have a J, oh wait I love this part. Isn't Nemo cute, he's got a bad fin, cause when he was a baby fish before he was borned, a shark ate his mom and his billion brothers and sisters, and he got hurted, and I asked mom if I could have a fish, but she said no, because they don't live berry long, but I said I would take good care of him, so maybe I'll get a Nemo for Christmas." She stared at him as if she was waiting for something. "Well, do you have a J?"

"Ohh no, go fish."

"'Kay," she said, pulling a card.

"Do you have a seven?" Chris asked.

"Go fish." She grinned. Looking over again at the television, Jocelyn's smile slipped away. "This is the sad part, Nemo gets taken by the diver and his dad tries to find him. If I got taken by a diver, my dad probably won't try to find me but that's okay," she said glancing down at her hand. "My mom said she would find me and that's all that matters. Do you gots a four?"

"Yes." Pulling the card out of his hand, Chris handed it to the beaming child. It amazed him she was able to have three conversations at once and share something so intimate all at the same time. Her father's lack of concern didn't even seem to faze her, nor did her mother's unconditional love seem to surprise her.

125

Taking the card from Chris's outstretched hand, Jocelyn grinned as if she had pulled the biggest coup in the land. "Told you I was good at this, Mr. Chris."

"I guess you did, kid."

They played and talked, or rather Jocelyn talked for a couple of more hands, before she began to fidget. Tossing the hand down, she asked. "You want to play something else?"

"It's amazing you want to play something else, now that I was finally in the lead," Chris teased.

"Nah, you would have lost anyway."

"Good to know, kid."

"Why do you keep calling me that?" she asked, leaning forward and resting her elbows on the table. Propping her face on her hands, she squinted up her nose at him.

"What?" he asked, sitting back against the couch to look at her cherub-like face.

"Kid. You done that lots tonight."

"I don't know," Chris shrugged. "Jocelyn seems like a lot of name for such a little tyke."

"I'm not little." Jumping to her feet, Jocelyn stood up big and tall to prove her point. "See I grow like a weed, at least that's what my papa says."

Standing, Chris looked over at her, towering several feet above her, and deepened his voice. "You're not that big."

"That's 'cause you're too big. I heard mom telling Aunt Veronica you were almost too big, but I've seen bigger. Governor Snortchingater is much bigger than you, he was at a rally my Uncle Robert took me too, and he was sooooo tall. He almost touched the sky."

Chris was taken back at the comment Jocelyn said about her mother telling her Aunt Veronica he was almost too big. The old adage that little pitchers have big ears never seemed so true as it did right now. He wondered if Eliza knew Jocelyn heard that little comment, because he was willing to bet when Eliza had said it, she hadn't been talking about his height.

Shaking his head, he smirked and sat back down on the couch. Jocelyn's attention had been drawn back to the screen and she was doing this little bop and chanting "Woo ha ha" along with the fish in the movie. Turning to him, she said, "You know what, you can call me Shark Bait, like in the movie. It can be your special name for me."

"Does 'kid' bother you that much?"

"Well, no, but it will be so cool. We can have secret identities, I'll be Shark Bait and you can be, umm, Gill."

"How come you get a cool name like Shark Bait and I get stuck with Gill?"

"Cause Gill is the coolest biggest fish in the tank. Come on, pleasseeeee," she begged, bouncing up and down.

Chris chuckled despite himself and nodded his head in agreement. "Alright, kid, from this moment on you'll be known as Shark Bait."

"Woo ha ha," Jocelyn chanted, bouncing up and down.

"And I'll be the coolest, baddest fish in the tank, Gill."

"Woo ha ha," she repeated again. Jumping on the couch, she tackled Chris in a big bear hug and squeezed with all her might. The hug surprised Chris, bringing back memories of another small girl who used to hug him.

"Thanks, Mr, I mean, Gill, it will be so much fun."

"Sure, Shark Bait, whatever you say." Chris patted her awkwardly on her back.

Pulling away, Jocelyn hopped off the couch and asked. "You want something to drink? 'Cause I'm thirsty."

"Sure."

"'Kay," she said, taking off for the kitchen. Chris glanced at the clock and wondered how much longer Eliza would be in the tub. He knew from experience it didn't take her that long to get off. She could have used both toys five times over by now. Standing, Chris headed down the hall, towards the bathroom, and paused outside of the door. Leaning forward a tad, he listened to see if he could hear anything. A buzz, a moan, a cry of fulfillment, anything to let him know what was going on it there.

"Do you gots to go potty?"

Chris jumped in surprise, and turned quickly around to see Jocelyn standing behind him, holding two juice boxes. "If you have to use it, you just knock on the door, and tell Momma you have to go."

"No, that's okay," he said, stepping away from the door.

"She don't mind." Walking past Chris, Jocelyn banged on the door with all her little might.

"Shark Bait, don't," Chris muttered, embarrassed. The last thing he wanted Eliza to know was he had been hanging outside her bathroom door like a pervert.

"Mom, Mr. Chris gots to go potty!" Jocelyn bellowed with all of her might.

"I'll be right out," Eliza called from behind the door.

"Okay, but hurry, cause I think he gots to go real bad 'cause he's standing outside the door."

"Oh really?"

Chris could hear the amusement leaking from her voice through the door. This was completely embarrassing, and looking down at Jocelyn, he could tell she thought she had done him a favor, by the way she was grinning at him.

"Thanks, Shark Bait," he said sarcastically.

"No problem, Gill." Handing him his juice, she took his free hand in hers and led him down the hall. "She'll be out in a minute, probably shaving her legs, it takes forever. She says I'll understand one day, but I don't get it. Want to see my room? It's over here. Momma decorated it for me in all Dora stuff. She's my favorite."

Tugging Chris into her room, she led him over to her tiny bed and pushed him backwards so he would sit down. And then she proceeded to bring out every single doll she owned and told him its name and who gave it to her. That led to an even longer discussion, all on her part, about who each person was and how they were related to her and how many kids they had.

By the time Eliza was standing in the doorway, Chris was convinced he could make a family tree just from the information Jocelyn had given him alone.

"The bathroom's free, Chris, if you still need to use it," Eliza teased from the doorway.

Her skin looked all flushed and rosy. Her dark hair was piled up high on her head and she was dressed in a pair of gray sweat shorts and matching T-shirt. In no way did she look like a woman bent on seduction, but she did have a very sleepy satisfied look in her eyes.

"I'm okay, thanks," he replied sheepishly. "Simple misunderstanding."

"Hmm." Eliza smiled. Turning to Jocelyn she said, "It's after eight, sweetie, bedtime."

"But, Mom, Gill is still here."

"Gill?" she questioned.

"It's a secret identity thing."

"Oh, I see. Well *Gill* will have to come back another time, Mami, its bedtime. You have soccer tomorrow."

"You want to come to my game tomorrow Gill?" she questioned, smiling up at him.

Chris didn't know what to say. In truth he could think of a thousand things he could be doing on Saturday, but the look in her eyes made him want to say yes.

"Mami, I'm sure Chris has other plans," Eliza said before he could even say anything.

Eliza's comment did two things. One, piss him off for assuming he would say no, although he was planning on it, and the other, make up his mind to go after all. It was one thing for him to find an excuse, but another for her to try to make up one for him.

"Of course I will, Shark Bait."

Jocelyn's squeal was loud enough to strip paint. Running past her mother, she grabbed on to Chris's legs and squeezed with all her little might. Looking down, Chris smiled and tousled her downy hair. Glancing across the room at Eliza, Chris chuckled inside at the shocked look on her face. Apparently, his answer shocked the hell out of her.

"All right, Mami, go brush your teeth, and say good night to Chris."

Looking up at him, Jocelyn smile and said, "Good night, Gill."

"Night, Shark Bait."

Running around him, Jocelyn headed down the hall to the bathroom.

"Why don't you wait for me in the living room?" Eliza said quietly.

Nodding, Chris walked into the living room and sat down on the couch. Laying his head back on the plush cushion, he closed his eyes, and wondered, not for the first time that night, what exactly he was doing there. Jocelyn was a cute kid, she could talk water up stream, but she was adorable nevertheless. Eliza was everything he could ever ask for in a woman, but it was always there in the back of his mind that his face wasn't the only thing he had inherited from his father.

Today at the office was a fine example. He lost his head, got jealous and started getting rough with her. What if something happened and he lost his temper with Jocelyn? He would never forgive himself if he hurt her or Eliza, but he couldn't stay away from her. He had even been willing to babysit tonight just so he could be near her.

"You're still in one piece I see," said Eliza, coming up from behind him. She paused at the lamp and dimmed it before walking over to the couch and sitting down next to him. She was holding a shoebox in one hand and the vanilla lotion in the other. Handing him the lotion, she laid her legs across his lap and leaned back, propping a pillow behind her.

"I didn't say I couldn't handle kids, just that I didn't want to get involved with them."

"Then what's with you going to the game?"

Pouring the lotion into his hands, he rubbed it between his palms and began to massage it into her smooth calves.

"She asked, I was being nice,"

"Well thanks." Looking over at him, she replied quietly, "Javier doesn't always get to make it, and my brothers and dad fill in whenever possible but they have their own families and lives. I guess she still hungers for a male figure."

"And what do you hunger for?" he asked, moving his fingers up her thighs.

"The bath was one of them."

"And how was it?"

"Orgasmic."

"Really." Slipping his hand in the loose opening of her shorts, Chris brushed his fingers across the silk edge of her panties.

"No, Chris."

"Why?"

"Just because Jocelyn went to bed doesn't mean she's asleep."

"So tonight was basically a punishment for me."

"No," she said, trying to pull her legs back, but he stopped her by gripping them. "Tonight was about me, not about punishing you."

"Which toy did you use?"

Blushing slightly, she picked up the shoebox off the ground and pulled out the Aqua Orb. "I tried the scrunchy thing too but this is what worked the best."

Taking it out of her hand, Chris brought it up to his nose and inhaled her faint scent off the vibrator. It smelt mainly of vanilla soap, but there was the slight hint of her on it. Enough to make his cock stir anyway.

"Let me ask you a question?" he asked softly.

"What?"

"Do you speak in Spanish when you come by yourself or only with me?"

Blushing hard, Eliza snatched her legs away and tucked them underneath her. Chris sprung at her, kissing her hard on the mouth. "I can't believe you're blushing over that."

"It's one thing to do it, it's another thing to talk about it."

"I think it's hot when you do it," he said, dropping a soft kiss on her slightly parted lips. "Say something to me now."

Licking her lips, she asked. "Like what?"

"I don't care, just make it dirty."

"Quiero mamarte ahora."

"What does that mean?"

"I want to suck your cock now," she replied huskily.

Groaning, Chris took her mouth under his and kissed her passionately. Slipping his tongue between her lips, he stroked her with it, like he wanted to stroke his hard cock in her. Pushing up against her, Chris froze when he heard in the distance a door opening. Pulling back quickly, he moved back to his side of the couch and counted to twenty, trying to calm his raging hormones down.

"Can I get some water, Mommy?"

"Jocelyn, you know better."

"Please I'm so thirsty, I might die if I don't get a drink."

Chris chuckled, realizing Eliza was right. There was no way they were going to do anything with Jocelyn in the apartment.

"A small glass and back to bed."

Standing, Chris watched Jocelyn dash into the kitchen and turned to Eliza. "I better get going."

"Okay." Picking up the shoebox, she handed it to him. "Take this home with you."

Looking over her shoulder at Jocelyn peeking out of the kitchen grinning, Chris took the box, no questions asked.

Walking to the door, he opened it. "I guess I'll see you tomorrow."

"If something comes up, don't worry about it."

"I told her I would go, so I will." Dropping a quick kiss on her lips, he said softy for her ears only, "But don't forget I get to go next."

Looking up, she smiled seductively, "That's what I'm counting on."

Chapter Eleven

The sun shone brightly over the soccer field on Saturday. The grass was bright green, and was being trampled by tiny feet running back and forth over it. No one really kicked the ball, more like kicked at it and at each other. But everyone was having fun, from the kids on the field to the parents on the sideline.

Jocelyn looked especially cute, thought a beaming Eliza. Her curly hair pulled back by a purple band, which matched her purple and white uniform. Her little knobby knees were anchored by long white socks, and she was running as fast as her tiny legs could manage.

The game was just getting underway when she felt a presence behind her chair. Turning around and looking up, she smiled in surprise at Chris who stood behind her. Even though he had said he was going to be there, she was a bit taking back to actually see him.

It was amazing to Eliza that even in the hot California weather, Chris still managed to look crisp and cool. He was casually dressed in jean shorts that looked freshly pressed and a light blue polo shirt. Chris looked like any of the preppy parents on the field. The only difference was that with the sizes of his muscular biceps, she'd bet he could probably out bench any of the men there.

"If you don't close your mouth, you're going to capture a fly in there," he teased, laughing down at her.

Smiling up at him, she replied, "What can I say? You amaze me."

Walking from behind her, Chris crouched beside her and took off his Sun Coast dark lens sunglasses. His light brown eyes twinkled brightly, and he seemed lighter, almost freer than she'd ever seen him.

"Amaze you, huh?"

"Yes, for a man who claims not to like kids."

"I never said that."

"You sure did come through for one little girl," she continued as if he hadn't interrupted her.

Chris's eyes darkened with concern. "Don't read more into this than there is, Eliza."

"Don't worry." She smiled, sadly running her fingers across his smooth brown cheeks. "I'm not, but thank you for coming. You're all she spoke about today."

Slipping his sunglasses back on, Chris stood up and put his hands in his pockets. Looking out to the field, he searched for Jocelyn and smiled when he finally saw her.

"She's got heart," he commented to Eliza.

"And that's all she has," she teased as Jocelyn kicked at the ball and missed. "She tries really hard. That's all that counts."

Looking down at Eliza, Chris asked, "Is her father here?"

"No." Reaching over, she grasped his pants pocket and pulled him closer to her. "But his mother will be coming afterwards to take her for the weekend."

"Really?"

"Yes."

"I guess it's my turn then," he teased.

"Well, I didn't wax for nothing," she replied, wiggling her brows.

Chris let out a purely masculine chuckle that sent shivers down her spine. "Words to warm a man's heart."

"I thought you would appreciate it."

"So what's the game plan?"

"Well, first Jocelyn's game and then you and I play?" she said seductively.

♦ ♥ ♣ ♠

The game was called after two hours, with Jocelyn's team winning by one point. It was hard to tell what she was more excited about, that her team had won or that Chris had come to watch. Bouncing all around him, she exuded happiness in a way that made Eliza happy and sad at the same time.

Javier wasn't as attentive as he could have been, but Eliza didn't know how much it bothered Jocelyn until now. The thing that worried Eliza the most though, was how attached Jocelyn was becoming to Chris. She could handle a broken heart a lot better than Jocelyn could. Eliza wondered just how much time she should allow Jocelyn to spend with Chris.

It would have been a lot easier if Jocelyn and Chris hadn't hit it off like they did, because no matter how much Chris wanted her now, Eliza couldn't shake the feeling he was still fighting some demons that would stop him from being happy with them.

After making sure Jocelyn got off okay with her grandmother, Eliza followed Chris over to his house in her car. He had wanted to drive, but Eliza wanted the freedom of leaving whenever she wanted. She could tell her need for independence bothered him, but she didn't care.

Pulling up to the ranch style tan house, Eliza looked around in awe. If the inside of the house was as lovely as the outside then Chris was a very lucky man. The lawn was immaculately cut, flowers bloomed in their beds and his house gleamed as if freshly painted. It was obvious Chris took pride in his surroundings, but she should have known that from the classy way his office looked.

Following him through the dark oak door, Eliza glanced around his hall before walking into the living room. A large brown suede couch dominated the room that was decorated in an Indian design. The walls had art placed strategically on it, with a beautiful Indian print woven rug, that she knew he didn't get from any carpet store.

"This is beautiful."

"Thank you," he said, carelessly tossing his keys on the glass tabletop. "I did it myself."

Gasping, she turned and stared at him in shock. The room looked like it could be in a model home or a floor model in some fancy boutique. "You're kidding me."

"No." Chris smiled, the pride in his voice evident.

"A man of many talents I see,"

"Many, and I'd like to show you a few right now."

Walking towards her, Chris had a devilish gleam in his eyes. Stopping in front of her, he began to pull the tangerine T-shirt she was wearing out of her shorts. "Last night was cold."

"No, it wasn't," she denied as he pulled her shirt over her head.

"Oh yes, it was." Tossing it on the floor, he reached for her tan shorts and began to unsnap them. "You came, I didn't. Even when I came home last night, I couldn't get myself off, because my hand couldn't grip me as tight as your pussy would. No amount of lotion was going to make it as wet as your mouth. Nothing was going to work but you. So I went to bed hard and aching, dreaming of the last thing you said to me before we said goodnight," he said as he walked her backwards to the couch.

"I'll be back," he huskily remarked, leaving the living room.

Eliza sat stunned on his couch. Chris's arousal was so strong she could taste it, and she wondered if he felt the same way. From the moment he started to speak, she became aroused. Now sitting alone in his living room, she was forcing herself to refrain from slipping her hands in her shorts to touch herself. Her nipples, hard and erect, scratched against the lace of her bra. Eliza tried to remember what she had said to him, but for the life of her, she couldn't remember it.

Chris entered the room dressed only in his black silk boxers, carrying the shoebox of toys she had given him last night. At the sight of the box in his hands, Eliza's pussy began to throb and ache from desire.

Walking in front of her, Chris opened the box, took out the Aqua Orb and handed it to her. Placing the box beside her on the couch, Chris stood with his hardened cock only inches from her waiting mouth.

"Do you remember what you said?"

"No," Eliza hoarsely murmured.

"Come on, think, baby." Chris dropped down in front of her and spread her thighs. Taking the orb from her, he placed the mini vibrator on the seam of her pants and turned it on. Even through the material of the shorts, Eliza could feel the vibrating motions on her pussy. "What did this innocent little mouth whisper to me in Spanish, right before I left?"

The words she said came back to her instantaneously. "*Quiero mamarte ahora.*"

"That's right, princess," he said, standing back up. "And that's what I want you to do."

Dropping his boxers to the ground, Chris stood in front of her, proud and erect. His cock jutted out in front of him, dark and large. The crown, darker in color than the rest of his cock, was a purplish black, thick and wide. Eliza reached out and grasped his thick member in her hand. Running her fingers slowly over the moist head, she ran her hand down the long length to his full round balls hanging between his parted legs.

Eliza took her time exploring him. Like a blind woman reading from Braille, she traced every curve and vein on him before finally slipping him into her mouth. Chris let out a harsh sound as she closed her lips around him. The feel of him in her mouth, so hard and so smooth was intoxicating to her.

Taking more of him in her mouth, Eliza swallowed as much of his cock as she could. His large member moved in and out of her hand, which was stroking his length as she sucked the top. Chris moved his hand behind her head, grabbing her hair and using it as a handle to fuck her face.

He let out a soft moan above her, his excitement as evident in sound as hers was in moisture. She was creaming her shorts just from sucking his cock. His flavor, his feel, his tight grip in the back of her hair had her on the verge of coming herself.

"I want you to use the orb as you suck me," Chris demanded between clenched teeth.

Pulling back, she took her mouth away from him as she kept up the steady rhythm of her hand. "I need to take my shorts off."

"No you don't," he said, pushing her mouth back to his waiting crown. "Use it through your shorts. You can still get off that way, it will just take longer."

Taking his cock back between her lips, Eliza grazed his head lightly with her teeth. Chris hissed at the sensation, but chuckled at her rebellion. Picking up the orb off the couch, Eliza pressed it hard into her wet mound and held it there with one hand while she stroked him with the other.

Pressing firmly against the orb, Eliza tried hard to concentrate on blowing him and getting off at the same time. The material of the shorts made it harder to feel the sensation of the vibrator, but as aroused as she was, she didn't need to feel all of the motion, just enough to get her off.

Picking up her speed, Eliza pressed harder into her clit and came, soaking her shorts in the process. Moaning in pleasure around his hard shaft, she had to restrain herself from biting down as the sensations coursed through her body.

"Watch it, baby," he teased, pulling out of her groaning mouth. "See, I knew you could do it."

Reaching into the box beside her, Chris took out a condom and slid it on as he dropped down in front of her. Pushing her back on the couch, he unbuttoned her shorts and pulled them, along with her wet panties, off her limp frame. Sliding his hands beneath her thighs, Chris draped Eliza's legs over his arms and pulled her forward until her ass was partially off the couch.

Slipping his hand between them, he placed the tip of his cock into her wet slit and pressed forward, groaning as he filled her.

"This is what I needed last night," he growled. "Inside you."

"Nothing else will do now," he said between thrusts. Sliding his hands down from her thighs, Chris latched onto her wrists, which lay on the couch gripping the cushion. Holding her down tightly, Chris powered into her, their bodies jerking into one another from the force of his thrusts.

Eliza tossed her head back and forth as the pleasure soared through her body. The feel of his powerful cock tunneling through her body made her scream with pleasure. Tugging on her arms, she reveled in the sensation of being held down and fucked, all at the same time. It was a complete high for her to be helpless, even if it was only temporarily. She never doubted for a moment he would hurt her, but the fact that he could do anything to her he wanted, was exciting.

"*Más duro*," she murmured, arching into him. "*Te necessito ahora.*"

Her words soon blended into inaudible sounds as Chris ground into her pelvis. Tapping with every stroke against her cervix, he caused her pleasure-pain sensors to go into over drive. Tilting her up a bit, Chris was able to pull her back onto him until her ass was bouncing against his thighs, spanking her cheeks with every thrust.

Eliza bit her lip to keep from screaming as his pace sped up and Chris bucked into her with all his might. Digging her nails into the cushion, Eliza pushed back into him, sobbing his name as she came around him.

Pounding into her, Chris groaned "fuck" as he thrust into her once more, coming as he shouted her name.

Letting go of her wrists, Chris pulled back and sat on his heels, looking up at an exhausted Eliza. She shook with ripples of pleasures still swimming through her body. Grabbing her thighs, Chris pulled her forward until she slid off the couch onto his lap and kissed her.

His tongue lapping against hers, Chris made love to her mouth, soft and gentle. Pulling away, Chris closed his eyes and rested his forehead on hers.

"You're going to be the death of me, woman."

"Hey, I just came over for lunch," she joked, laying her head back on his couch.

Bending forward, Chris ran his lips over her throat, kissing her exposed flesh. "We're a complete mess."

"Shower?"

"Oh yes, my nozzle is handheld, I can't wait to get you in there."

"Isn't your turn up yet?" Rolling her head over to the side, she smiled up at him.

"No, that was just the first round."

Tired and achy, Eliza scooted out of Chris's bed as carefully and as quietly as she could. It was going on six pm and she wanted to be home, in case Jocelyn called. Although she had given Marie, her former mother-in-law, her cell number, she still wanted to be available for Jocelyn.

They had made love more times than she could count. In every position imaginable and even some she had never imagined. Chris was tireless in his passion, and insatiable. If she died tonight, she would have to say she would die a happy, satisfied woman. He was everything she had always dreamed of and more.

Dressing in the living room, she looked around for anything she might have left. Walking around the room, she looked at the family photos on his fireplace and smiled at the pictures of him as a young boy. Picking one up, she ran her finger lovingly around his features and wondered if they had a child what features he or she would get from him.

Setting the frame back down, she picked up one of a beautiful dark skinned black woman, who resembled Chris slightly. She had his eye color and his full lips. She smiled amusedly at the camera with a look of adoration in her eyes. The picture seemed as if taken by a loved one and not in a studio, because of her non-staged smile. Thinking back to the name on his chest, Eliza wondered if this was Tay, his little sister.

"What are you doing?" Chris asked, walking up from behind her.

Placing the photo back on the shelf, she turned and smiled. "Just looking at your photos. Is that your sister?"

"Yes." Taking her hand, he tried to pull her gently yet firmly away from the fireplace, but Eliza was having none of it. Digging her feet in, she stood where she was and yanked her hand away.

"She's very pretty," she commented stubbornly. She wasn't going to let him pull away from her.

Looking at her, frowning, he asked, "Yes, she is. Are you going somewhere with this?"

"Do you have a problem talking about your family?"

"No. I just don't want to."

"Is your goal to pick a fight every time we make love?"

"I'm not trying to pick a fight with you, Eliza, I'm just private when it comes to my family."

"But I'm not a stranger, Chris. I'm the same woman you just spent half the day making love to."

"I know," he said, frustrated. "Look, there are just some things I would rather not talk about. Okay?"

"Fine." Eliza walked over to the couch and picked up her purse. "I have to go."

"Why?"

"I need to get home in case Jocelyn calls."

"Call her and give her the number here."

"That's not a good idea," she said, walking around him, heading for the door.

"Why not?" Chris asked, stepping in front of her.

"Because it isn't." Stepping up on her tiptoes, she kissed him on his lips quickly and reached for the door.

"Are you leaving because I won't answer your questions?"

"No." Turning, she smiled sadly up at him. "I'm leaving because I have a five-year-old daughter who needs to know I'll be home to say goodnight to her when she calls. But most importantly, I'm leaving because I had a wonderful day with you and I don't want to end it on a bad note."

"What about Fantasy Number Two?"

"Are you going to do it, no matter what it is?"

"Does it involve sex this time?"

"Does it matter?"

Frowning he sighed, "No, I guess not."

"Do you have a piece of paper I can write it down on?"

"Just tell me."

"No, I want you to read it when I'm gone and call me later tonight and let me know if you will do it."

"This is juvenile, you know?" he grumbled, stomping out of the room.

Eliza chuckled softly at his retreating back. He was so childlike it wasn't funny. She had never seen someone so capable of love, yet not know how to express it, in her entire life. All day long, he had made sure she was okay. He catered to her every need, even asking if she wanted to check in on Jocelyn several times. Yet when things came up that had to do with him and his emotions, he froze her out.

Walking in, he thrust the paper and pen at her and grumbled behind her as she wrote. Folding it up, she handed it to him, and kissed him again, this time taking her time to linger before pulling away.

"Call me and let me know."

"If the answer is no, then what?"

"Then the answer is no." She shrugged and opened the door.

"Is our seeing each other dependent on whether my answer is yes or no?"

"But we're not seeing each other. Right, Chris? We're just fucking." Stepping out of the door, Eliza pulled it closed behind her, smiling slightly when she heard him swear behind her.

Chapter Twelve

There was a reason gambling was illegal, Chris thought with frustration, looking down at the cookbook in front of him. He should have never made a sucker bet with Eliza, without clearing up a few basic rules.

Rule Number One should have been all fantasies have to be sexually pleasurable for two. No masturbating in the tub, unless he could watch. Rule Number Two, no fantasies that didn't include sex. Sure it was similar to the first rule, but getting fucked should definitely be spelled out in every rule.

If those two rules had been in place from the beginning, he wouldn't be playing Benson and hopping through her fucking hoops like a show dog. All this, just so he could get some trim. They weren't supposed to be having a relationship, they were only supposed to be fucking. Fucking like monkeys, wild-and-crazy-hanging-from-trees sex. None of this talking about your emotions bullshit.

The phone ringing pulled him away from his silent rant. Wiping his hand on a towel, he picked up the phone and bellowed, "What?"

"Well, how the hell are you, too?" teased a soft voice on the other line.

"Sorry, Tay, I'm kind of preoccupied."

"I'd say," Octavia quipped back. Her amusement trickled over the line, easing some of the tension from his shoulders. "What are you up to?"

"Cooking dinner." he grumbled.

"And that has you so upset?"

"You need to explain something to me."

"If I can."

"Why are women so damn confusing?"

"Are we talking about a particular woman or women in general?"

"If someone offered to fulfill three of your fantasies, would you include one of them as food and conversation?"

"I guess it depends on what you're planning on doing with the food, and what you're talking about?" Tay teased.

"See, now that's just wrong," Chris groaned.

"I need more details."

"Okay, listen to this." Grabbing the note off the counter, Chris opened it and read from it. "For my second fantasy, I want you to cook me a homemade meal and have a conversation with me. I want to be able to ask you anything I want, and in return, you can ask me anything you want, and we both have to be honest. Dinner and conversation."

"Ohhh."

"Exactly. Now what kind of fantasy is that?" he demanded.

"Well, I can see how getting a man to be open and honest with me could be a fantasy come true."

"You're on my side, remember?"

"I didn't know it was a side thing. You got to let me know these things, bro."

"She's driving me crazy. She's annoying and pushy and she has a kid."

"And..."

"She's beautiful, kind and sexy as all get out, and Jocelyn is a great kid."

"So her only problem is she has whacked fantasies."

"No," he growled into the phone. "The problem is Eliza doesn't know how to let shit go. She wants to keep probing and probing until she eats at the center of me."

"Chris..." Tay sighed.

The doorbell rang before he could continue. "Look, she's here, got to go. I'll talk to you later, Tay."

"Chris..."

But he hung up the phone, interrupting her last comment. Turning the oven off, Chris walked out of the kitchen and down the hall to the door.

Eliza was dressed as if they were eating out, in a spaghetti strapped, skintight black dress, and black heels. She was holding lilies out to him, the same kind he had brought to her the other night.

Stepping in, she handed him the flowers and kissed him on the cheek. "Something smells delicious."

"Thanks," he said dryly, looking down at the flowers. He had never been given flowers before and it felt somewhat strange. Good but strange nevertheless. "You look good enough to eat."

"The night is young," she teased, tossing her hair over her shoulder. "How long until dinner?"

Raising a brow, he asked, "Ready to get the inquisition started?"

"No, I just wanted to know how long I had to hold my stomach in. This dress is cute, but it doesn't hide a thing."

"Go sit at the table, and I'll bring everything out." Gesturing to the dining room, Chris headed back into the kitchen and placed the flowers in a vase. Taking the roast out of the oven, Chris sliced into it and placed it onto the serving tray.

After bringing all the food out to the table, Chris sat down in his chair and faced Eliza as if ready to do battle. Much to his surprise, during dinner she made small talk, asking random things like where he learned to cook and casual stuff like that. When he cleared the table and brought out the coffee and cheesecake he had purchased, he had relaxed enough to move his chair down closer to hers and enjoy himself some.

Picking up her coffee, Eliza asked "So tell me about your sister?"

Stiffening, Chris lowered his raised cup. "What about her?"

"I don't know." She shrugged. "How old is she, what does she do, where does she live? The usual."

"Tay is twenty five, a social worker and she lives in Los Angeles."

"That wasn't so hard now, was it?"

Chris didn't answer, just stared at her, waiting for her to continue. Sighing, Eliza laid her cup down and reached over to touch his clenched hand. "This is getting-to-know-you stuff; it shouldn't be so hard to answer."

"It isn't." Pulling his hand away from under hers, Chris tried to distance himself emotionally from the conversation.

"Look, I'll go. I have three brothers, Joseph, Anthony and Robert. Joseph is thirty-three, married with two kids, a boy and a girl. Anthony is thirty-one, a lawyer and single, and Robert is twenty-nine, married and expecting his first child any day now." Pushing her cup away, she asked, "Now was that so hard?"

"Why do you want to know these things?"

"Because I want to know you."

"I'm right here."

"No, you're not, your body is, but you're not. You're wound so tight that one wrong move and you're going to snap."

"Well, then maybe you shouldn't be here when I do," he said through gritted teeth.

"Damn it, Chris, I just want to know you."

"My past isn't important."

"It is when it reflects on your future."

"It doesn't."

"Why don't you want kids?"

"What's that have to do with anything?"

"Do you like Jocelyn?"

"I think she's a great kid," Chris admitted.

"Can you imagine being around to watch her grow up, being a part of her day-to-day life?" Eliza asked, her voice hopeful.

"I'm not father material." Looking down, Chris stared at his tightly clenched fist, an image so familiar to the way he had seen his father's so many times before.

"Why?" Leaning over, she asked gently, "Did you have a bad childhood?"

Chris refused to answer. Voices in his head cried out in anger, images of Tay crying on soiled sheets filled his head. Memories of another life came crashing back.

"What did you go to juvie for?" Eliza asked, frustrated at his silence. Taking his silence as dismissal, Eliza got angry. "Damn it, Chris, why won't you open up to me?"

"What do you want to know, damn it? Do you want to know that I got busted when I was thirteen for stealing a stereo, so I could sell it for money."

"If that's the truth, then yes."

"You want some more truth, how about this? Before that, Tay and I lived with a nineteen-year-old drug dealer, who basically bought us from our parents for crank."

"Oh God, Chris," Eliza said, tears filling her emerald eyes.

"Oh don't feel sorry for us, it was the best thing that ever happened to us. My father was an abusive drunk on his good days and a violent crackhead on his bad days. And my mother was just as bad. The nicest memory I have of my childhood is living with a thug named D Dog who taught me how to cook coke and who fed me and my sister on a regular basis for two years before he was shot in a deal gone bad. The lowlifes you see criminalized on the news treated us better than our own fucking flesh and blood. And when I got busted three months later, Tay was taken and put in foster care. I didn't know where she was for eighteen months."

Pulling his shirt over his head, Chris grabbed her hand, placed it over his tattoo and held it there forcefully. "And I traded a pack of smokes and my dessert for this tattoo because I thought I wouldn't see her again. But I got out. I tracked her down, and thanks to some good people and a social worker who was willing to pull some strings, we were able to stay together."

"Chris, that's nothing to be ashamed of." Tears streaming down her face, Eliza tried to pull him to her.

"I'm not ashamed," he denied, pushing her hand off him and standing up. "Does this story work for you?

Some women get off on the thug life. Is that what you want, Eliza, a roughneck?"

"I want you, Chris. All of you, the good and the bad." Standing, she walked to him and tried to put her arms around him.

Chris pushed her away, stepping out of her reach. "There isn't any good, Eliza, that's what I'm trying tell you."

"That isn't true, I see the good in you."

"Really? When? Was it when I got pissed off at you at work and threw you against the wall?"

"No, it was when you let my daughter call you Gill, and you showed up at her soccer game. It's the way you are with Dylan and Kayla, and with me. The tattoo on your chest that says your sister's name. These are things that prove you have a heart."

Shaking his head, he turned to walk away.

Eliza called out to him, stopping him in his tracks. "Do you care for me?"

Chris froze, unsure of what to say. His heart pounded and he clenched his hands at his side. Without turning around, he said softly, "You know I do."

"Then tell me."

Gritting his teeth, he turned around and looked at Eliza. Her face wet with tears looked at him, imploring him to love her back. "I just did."

"I love you, Chris." Walking towards him, she took his hand in hers. "Can you say the same thing?

Emotions coursed through him. Anger, fear, love, all bottled inside of him. Chris took the easy way out and grabbed the emotion he was most familiar with. Anger. "Is this a test, another fucking hoop I have to jump through?" he asked, snatching his hand away.

"No, it's a question. Do you love me?" Eliza asked sadly. Chris could tell his silence was hurting her but he didn't know what to do. Eliza turned to walk away, and Chris panicked. He knew, deep down inside, that if she left she wouldn't ever come back. Walking behind her, he gripped her shoulders and spun her around.

"So is this it?" he demanded. "Is your fucking little fantasy over?"

"Yes," she choked out.

"Great." Picking her up, he put her on the table and swept the dishes to the ground. "That means it's my turn."

Crushing her mouth under his, Chris pushed up her dress over her thighs, moving it out of his way. Part of him wanted her to fight him, to prove to himself he was evil, like he always thought he was, but to his surprise, Eliza began to respond. Wrapping her arms around his neck, Eliza pulled up on him, helping him ease her panties down her thighs.

Chris stepped back to toss them on the floor and opened his slacks. Eliza used the opportunity to grab her dress and pull it off, freeing her breasts to his greedy eyes and hands. Taking out his cock, Chris looked down and watched as his thick glistening shaft parted her bare lips and slid into her heated core. Fighting back the urge to close his eyes and enjoy the sensation, Chris forced his eyes to stay opened and zeroed in on her full breasts bouncing as he pushed into her.

The feel of his bare cock made him freeze for a moment. He had never, ever fucked without a condom before, but he didn't want to stop. He knew this might be the last time they ever had sex again, and he wanted to feel every minute of it bareback.

Chris moved his hand up her stomach and cupped her full breast, squeezing it, rubbing his thumb over her erect nipple. Taking her nipple in his hand, he twisted between his fingers as he leaned forward and took the other one in his mouth. Eliza groaned and grasped his head tighter to her body. When her muscles tightened inside, signaling her orgasm, Chris could actually feel it rock her body. Her body squeezed and milked his cock as she shook with pleasure.

Tearing his mouth away from her nipple, Chris grasped her hips and moved deeper inside her. Not wearing a condom was definitely better than wearing one, Chris thought as he fucked her pussy with deep long strokes, running his sensitive head inside her quivering body. It was like nerve endings he never knew he possessed tingled and came alive. The feel of only her surrounding him was like nothing he had ever known. The difference was amazing.

Slowing down to control his need, Chris slipped his hand under her to grip her ass and ran his fingers in her crack. Eliza cried out at the feel of his finger grazing her rosette. Chris ran his finger down between them where their juices spilled out and transported some of her sweet nectar to her rosette, teasing her puckered hole with his fingertips. Her body convulsed, this time dragging him along with her. Chris felt his balls tighten, and his thighs shake from the pressure of his oncoming release.

"Tell me," he growled to her as he pumped into her faster.

"I love you, Chris," she cried. " Te amo, te amo, te amo."

Seconds before Chris released his grasp on his control, he pulled out spraying her stomach with his seed. Jerking his cock in a fast motion, he emptied his spurting cock on her waiting flesh. Chris's body shook with the aftermath of his orgasm. Never before had he felt so overwhelmed during and after sex than he had at this moment.

Easing up from between Eliza's quivering thighs, he stepped back and looked down at her. Her body was shivering. From chill or shock, he couldn't tell, but other than that, she seemed okay. Chris didn't know what he would do if he hurt her. Hell, he didn't want to even think about the possibility of it.

Blindly he reached to the side, grabbed part of the tablecloth and wiped at the mess he had made on her stomach. Eliza's hand settled on top of his, and she gave him a soft squeeze. The comforting gesture was more than he could take. Chris snatched his hand back, causing Eliza to look up at him with a slight frown.

"The shower's down the hall." he muttered as he stepped away from her. The words came out harsher than he intended, but he couldn't help it. He needed to get away from her before he did something stupid like drop down on his knees and beg her for her forgiveness.

"Chris..." Eliza began, but he just shook his head and walked out of the room.

Chris waited outside the bathroom for Eliza to get out of the shower. He had already cleaned up their mess, or he should say his mess, off the table and the floor. After that power fuck, all he wanted to do was to crawl under the table and sleep, but real life was never that easy. After the orgasm came the guilt, and it was eating away at his soul like acid.

He started to walk away but turned when the door opened up behind him. Eliza looked shocked to see him there. "What's with you and bathrooms?" she teased gently.

"I was just trying to make sure you were okay." Reaching out his hand, he caressed the side of her face.

"Of course I am, Chris," she said, smiling, leaning her head into his hand.

"I think we should talk."

"Isn't that why I was here in the first place?" she kidded.

Nodding, he dropped his hand, turned, walked down the hall and entered the living room. Standing next to the fireplace, Chris tensed up when he felt Eliza touch his back.

"I don't think we should continue with this anymore," he said quietly.

"Why?"

Turning to face her, he said, "Because, Eliza, I damn near raped you in the dining room."

"You did not," she denied. "I was right there with you the whole time."

"But don't you see, when I get angry I turn into him. And the last thing in the world I want to do is hurt you, or Jocelyn."

"Do you think it won't hurt us when you walk away?"

"That will heal quicker than a bruise."

Sighing, Eliza shook her head sadly. "You really don't know, do you, Chris? You could be so happy with us. I could make you so happy."

"I can't risk it."

Chris watched as anger filled her eyes.

"You're a fucking coward, Chris. And you're not backing away from me or from our deal. You owe me one more fantasy."

"Eliza, I can't…"

"You can and you will."

"What do you want from me?" he demanded.

"You." Turning away, she scooped up her purse off his couch and stormed out of his house.

Chris watched her leave and prayed it wasn't for the last time.

Chapter Thirteen

Eliza sat at her desk, tired and exhausted. She felt as if she had been dragged behind a tow truck kicking and screaming, all night long. She had thought that last night was the worst night of her life, but she was wrong. Today Chris was acting as if nothing had ever happened between them at all.

She was back to being Mrs. Rivera, something he hadn't called her since she had started temping, over seven months ago. Eliza wasn't sure she could stay in this situation. She loved him, she really did, but she wouldn't sit by pining after him when it was obvious he didn't want anything to do with her. If he could be this cold less than twenty-four hours after they had last made love, then she could only imagine how ruthless he would be in a week or a month.

Glancing at the clock on her computer, she saved the file she was working on and logged out. Javier was going to drop Jocelyn off soon, and she wanted to get out of there before Jocelyn saw Chris. It was one thing for her to pine after him, but it was something completely different for her daughter to.

She heard Jocelyn's laughter seconds before they came into view. Closing her cabinet drawer, she placed an envelope in her pocket and walked in front of her desk, bending over just as Jocelyn came running over into her work area.

"Hi, Momma," Jocelyn said, throwing herself in Eliza's arms. Hugging and squeezing her, Eliza welcomed her back. Looking up, Eliza smiled at Javier. He looked suave as usual, dressed in gray slacks and a white button up shirt.

At five nine, Javier was more lanky than tall, with wavy dark brown hair and smooth almond colored skin. Javier was just as attractive today as he had been when they met in college so many years ago. The only difference between now and then was that he was older, unfortunately not wiser.

In many ways, Javier was still childlike, and like a child he could be charming and mischievous, but also very undependable. This was what they seemed to argue about the most. Eliza knew he loved Jocelyn. He doted on her since the time she was born, but he was never there when it mattered.

"Did you have fun, Mami?" she asked, looking into Jocelyn's upturned smiling face.

"Yes, but I missed you."

"I missed you too." Giving her an extra squeeze, Eliza stood back up, turned to Javier and asked, "How are you doing?"

"Great." He gave her his full wattage smile. "You're looking good."

"Thanks."

The door opened to Chris's office and he walked out carrying a folder, pausing in mid-stride when he saw Javier and Jocelyn. When Jocelyn saw him, her face lit up. Grinning from ear to ear, she left Eliza's side and ran to Chris's. Wrapping her arms around his legs, she looked up at him with pure adoration on her little face. "Hey, Gill."

"Hi, Shark Bait," he replied, smiling down at her. With his free hand, he patted her back, squeezing her into his leg.

Eliza looked on sadly. It was very obvious by the way he looked at Jocelyn that he cared for her. Any fool could see it. That was unless the fool was Chris Wilson.

The smile faltered from Javier's face when he saw the way Jocelyn responded to seeing Chris, but he quickly recovered and walked over to them, smiling his typical charming smile. Javier was accustomed to being the center of attention, so Jocelyn's reaction wasn't something he liked, and it was apparent from the way he cockily approached Chris.

Walking over to Chris, Javier held his hand out to him, smiling. "Hi, Chris, I'm Javier, Jocelyn's father. I must have heard a million things about you."

Looking down at his hand, Chris ignored it and replied, "Really, because I haven't heard anything about you." Patting Jocelyn on the back protectively, he continued, "You missed a really good game on Saturday."

His smile faltering, Javier lowered his hand. "Well, I'm sure I did, but something came up."

"I doubt anything so important that you couldn't have rescheduled." Looking down at Jocelyn, he said to her. "Shark Bait, do you think you can run into my office and look on my desk for a red folder?"

"Sure, Gill," she said, leaving his embrace and running into the office.

Walking behind her, Chris shut the door and turned back to Javier, frowning. "Nothing, and I mean nothing, should be more important than being there for her."

Walking over to Chris, Eliza placed her hand on his lower back, rubbing him softly. She wanted to calm him down before he got too riled up. Although it was nice to have him on her side, she didn't want him upsetting himself. After their conversation last night, she knew he was speaking from experiences, not just from observation. "It's okay, Chris," she said soothingly.

"No, it isn't."

"Look, man, I don't know what you've heard about me, but I think you've got me all wrong."

"No, I think I understand you completely. You have a beautiful little girl in there who wants to spend time with you, *now*. But there will come a time, I assure you, when she won't. She needs to know that if she gets taken by divers you'd move heaven and earth to find her."

"Divers? What are you talking about?"

"That's my point exactly," Chris firmly pointed out as his office door opened. Jocelyn ran out, carrying the red folder he had requested.

"Here you go, Gill, I found it." Looking up at him, smiling, she handed him the folder.

"Thanks Shark Bait." Turning to Eliza, Chris said, "I need to speak with Dylan, but I need to see you before you go."

Winking down at Jocelyn, Chris left the office with three pair off eyes staring at his back. Eliza and Jocelyn's adoring, and Javier's confused.

"What was that all, about?" Javier asked puzzled.

Shaking her head, Eliza turned to him and smiled patiently. "That's the point, Javier, you don't even have a clue." Gesturing to Javier, Eliza nudged Jocelyn. "Give daddy a kiss, Mami, so he can go."

Running over, Jocelyn gave him a brief kiss before running back to Eliza's side. Jocelyn's disinterest in him was sad, but not of her own making. Eliza knew Chris was right, if Javier didn't watch out Jocelyn wasn't going to want him in her life at all.

"I'll see you in two weeks," Javier said, dazed at the turn of events.

Nodding her head, Eliza watched him leave, feeling sad for him. He made his bed, now he would definitely have to lie in it.

"Mom, can I go sit in your chair and play?" Jocelyn asked hopefully.

"That's fine," Chris said, walking back into the office.

Jocelyn squealed in happiness and hopped on the chair.

"I know you were getting ready to leave, but could you fax this over to RLS before you go?"

"Sure." Taking the papers from his hand, Eliza turned to the fax machine behind her desk. "Thanks, by the way for what you said to Javier."

Snorting, he crossed his arms over his chest. "I doubt it will do any good."

Looking over her shoulder at him, she replied "Me too, but still I appreciated what you said."

"I know you probably won't believe me, but I care about what happens to you."

"I believe you, Chris." Turning around to face him, she said, "You just don't care enough."

"Damn it," he swore softly. Taking her arm, he shuffled them into his office and out of view of the door. Moving away from Eliza, Chris turned and looked at her helplessly. "This is all I'm capable of, Eliza."

"You're capable of so much more." Unable to help herself, Eliza went to him, needing to touch him once more. "And I need so much more."

Stepping back, he pulled away from her. "Well, I hope you find it."

"So do I." Smiling sadly, she reached into her pants pocket and pulled out the envelope she had placed in there. "This is for you."

Looking down at the letter frowning, Chris asked suspiciously, "What is it?"

"My letter of resignation."

"I'm not taking that."

Walking over to his office door, she closed it so they wouldn't be heard. "I'm giving you three weeks' notice, leaving me a week to train anyone you like."

"Did you hear me?" he demanded angrily. "I'm not taking that fucking note."

"I wasn't asking your permission," she stated calmly.

"You called me a coward." Grabbing her arm, he gripped her tightly. "What do you call this move you're making?"

"Smart."

"How is it smart? Do you have another job lined up? Are you prepared financially to make this move?"

"No, but I have to."

"You said you loved me, did that just go away?"

"No, of course it didn't."

"Then explain something to me then. How do you say you love me last night, and today tell me you're leaving?" Chris's frustration level was high. His eyes glimmered with pain and anger, and his face was flushed.

Bringing her arms up, Eliza placed them on his forearms and squeezed him gently. Chris released his hold on her and stormed to his desk, swiping his hand across it.

"Did you or didn't you not just moments ago tell me you hope I will be able to find what it is I'm looking for?" she questioned from behind him. How dare he treat this as if it was her fault? He was the one telling her to go, at the same time he was trying to hold on to her.

"So I have to lose my secretary because I can't say I love you."

"Are you really that cold and unfeeling?"

Chris flinched as if she had hit him. "This was a mistake."

"Well, now I'm correcting it."

A buzz from his intercom caused them both to turn and look at his desk in surprise. "Gill, you gots a visitor." Jocelyn's voice boomed over the speaker as if she was shouting into the box.

Eliza turned and opened the door, hurrying out into the outer office. "I'm so sorry," she apologized to the woman smiling down at Jocelyn. "Can I help you with anything?"

The woman turned and looked up at her with eyes just like Chris's. Eliza immediately recognized her from the picture on his mantel. "Yes, I'm here to see my brother."

With high cheekbones, full lips and skin the color of dark mocha, Tay Wilson was very attractive. So attractive that if she were a bit taller she could have been a model. Eliza could tell that despite their parenting skills, Chris and Tay's parents must have been attractive people to bear two breathtakingly beautiful kids as they had.

"You must be Tay."

Laughing, she stuck out her hand and replied, "Octavia, please. Chris is the only one that calls me that."

"Sorry," Eliza apologized, feeling a bit embarrassed.

"Is this your daughter?"

"Yes."

"She's very beautiful and very smart. She told me she was in charge because you two were in a meeting," Octavia said, her voice full of laughter.

"She catches on fast."

"I can tell."

Chris stepped out of his office with a surprised smile on his face. "Tay, what are you doing here?" he asked, embracing her in a huge bear hug.

"I was in the neighborhood."

The two siblings hugged each other as if they hadn't seen each other in a while. The distance might have been great between them but the love wasn't. It radiated off them like a bright sunrise, big and beautiful. More so, now that Eliza knew what they had gone through together.

"I met your new secretary," she teased. "The little one, not the tall one."

Ending their hug, Chris pulled back, arm still around her waist, anchoring Octavia to him. Smiling over at Jocelyn, he remarked jokingly, "Real efficient, isn't she?"

"What's 'ficient?" Jocelyn asked, scrunching up her nose.

"It means you're really good at your job."

"Yep, I'm very 'ficient at Mommy's job. I can help her all the time."

"I'd ask for a raise if I were you." Octavia winked.

"Hey, you take care of your staff and I'll take care of mine."

Eliza looked at them, feeling slightly sad. There were so many things she wanted to ask Octavia but now wasn't the time, not that there ever would be. Clasping her hands on Jocelyn's shoulder, she said, "Well, we're off. It was nice meeting you."

The happiness flew out of Chris's eyes, and he stiffened up. Letting go of his hold on Octavia, he stepped closer to her. "Our conversation isn't over," he stated, his voice lowering.

Eliza smiled a false smile and replied, "As far as I'm concerned it is."

"Eliza," he growled.

"Tomorrow."

Stepping back, he nodded his head, and Eliza knew this conversation was in no way over.

"I'll see you later, Shark Bait."

"Later, Gill. Later, Tavia."

Without another word, Eliza picked up her purse and turned to leave. Walking down the hall, she paused when she heard Chris's voice boom out from behind her. "Tomorrow, Eliza." Continuing down the hall, Eliza seriously considered calling in sick tomorrow.

Chapter Fourteen

"So why do I feel like I just walked in on something?" Octavia asked as Chris turned back around frowning

"What do you mean?"

"Is she last night's whacked fantasy woman?"

"Also known as Eliza, the bane of my existence."

"So what did this evil woman do?"

"She told me she loved me."

"I'm going to go kick her ass right now, hold my purse." Taking off her purse, she slipped out of her pumps, forcing Chris to see past his anger and laugh, which is what she had been going for.

"You don't have to take off your Manolos," he said smiling.

"You know me, any reason to step out of these things is a good one to me."

"Are your dogs barking?" he asked, referring to her feet. Walking into his office, Chris held the door open for her as she limped in.

"Like you wouldn't believe," she answered. Hobbling over to a couch, she sat down and waited until Chris sat next to her before she propped her feet up on his lap and wiggled her toes. "Why do women wear these things?"

"You're a woman, you're supposed to know."

"You bought them for me."

"Only after you begged me."

"You're older, you should know better," she bantered back. "I've missed you, knucklehead."

"You should come home more often."

"Work."

"You work too hard," he grumbled, rubbing her feet.

"Coming from a workaholic like you, I'll take it as a compliment." Sighing, she relaxed into his massage and laid her head back on the couch. "So what's going on, brother of mine? Because I cut out of work and left Jason in charge, and you know how I feel about that."

"He's still working there? I'm surprised he hasn't quit yet."

"You and me both, he's surprising me I have to say."

"I don't like the tone in your voice," he growled, squeezing her feet tightly.

"Ouch!" Snatching her feet off his lap, she rubbed them, complaining, "I was just saying, I'm surprised he's still around."

"It was the way you said it."

"How?"

"Like you're interested in him."

"And that would be the end of the world because..."

"Tay, don't do that to me. My heart can't take it."

"There are worst things in the world than to end up with a white man, and besides, unless Eliza is extremely high yellow, she ain't black."

"No, she isn't, but this isn't about me."

"Well, let's make it about you. What's going on? Looks like there was trouble in Whoville when I came in."

"Nothing," he grumbled, slouching back in the couch.

"She seemed really nice, and her daughter looks like a doll."

"They're both great."

"But..."

"You know my rule."

"You're not still working with that jacked up rule, are you?"

"You more than anyone should know it's there for a reason.

"What reason, Chris?"

"Don't you start, Tay."

"Look, I'm not afraid of your black ass, so try that bull with someone who gives a damn."

"I don't want to talk about this."

"And I don't care." Sighing, she leaned forward and placed her hand on his arm. "Chris, you've been alone and unhappy for so long. I could tell in your tone last night, and by the way you were acting today, that you care for her."

"I can't risk them."

"Risk them to what?"

"To me, damn it."

Octavia threw back her head and laughed. Looking up, she giggled even more at the look of annoyance on his face. "I've never met a less dangerous man in my life."

"You don't know what you're talking about."

"If there's someone more knowledgeable on the subject of you, I'd like to meet them."

"Maybe you don't remember what it was like growing up there Tay, but I do."

"Of course I remember, Chris," her voice lowered sympathetically.

"Then you might remember what they were like. What the fists felt like, the way their voices could make the hair on your arm stand up." Getting off the couch, Chris walked over to the window in his office and looked out.

The setting sun seemed like an abstract painting on the horizon. Colors littered the sky like a spilt bottle of paint, but the only thing Chris could see was the images of fists flying. His body shook with the flashback of his childhood. Chris gripped the table in front of him, steadying himself under the onslaught of pictures rumbling through his mind.

"I couldn't live with myself if I hurt them," he said quietly, his voice shaking with pain.

"She didn't seem so happy a few minutes ago."

"You know what I mean, Tay."

"I do." Standing, she followed him to the other side. "But, Chris, if anybody knows how not like them you are, it's me."

"But..."

"Chris, you have to move past it. You're no more like our father than I'm like our mother." Laying her hand softly on his arm, Octavia looked deep in his eyes. "If you cut yourself off from the rest of the world, you'll never heal. They'll win, Chris, and we can't let them. Forgive them and move on, or you'll never be happy."

Snorting he said, "You make it sound so easy."

"It is." Tugging on his arm until he looked down at her, Octavia said, "Forgive them."

"Never."

"You have to."

"Why?"

"Because look at you. You're a successful beautiful man, who lives alone. You never let people in. I'm really surprised you and Dylan are still friends, to tell you the truth."

"He wouldn't go away," Chris joked, trying to lighten the mood, but Octavia was having none of that.

"And neither will I, and from the looks of Eliza, neither will she."

"Yeah right, that's why she tried to give me her resignation."

"Give her a reason to stay."

"I can't think of any," he said sadly.

"Really? I can think of one."

"What?"

"You love her."

Chris didn't say anything, just looked back out the window.

Octavia sighed and laid her head on his shoulder. "You do, don't you?"

"Yes,"

"Can you imagine not being with her? Not being with Jocelyn?"

"I can, because it's best for them."

"How can it be best for them to not be with you?"

"All that shit we went through, Tay, it's handed down like a tacky tablecloth. All wrapped up like some nasty family heirloom, waiting for me to dish out to them. No matter what Pops taught me, or how good they treated us, I'm still Christopher Davis's son. I see that son of a bitch every time I look in the mirror. I feel him in me when I get pissed off, when I see a bottle of Jack, when I smell cheap cologne. I see him waiting to come out. And I won't give that little girl nightmares like you used to have for years."

"And who woke up and sat with me when I did?" Tears filled her eyes, making them shine like new pennies. "Who taught me how to tie my shoe, how to ride a bike, and much to Mama's dismay, about the birds and the bees? You did, Chris."

Chuckling through the tears clogging his throat, Chris remembered that very matter of fact conversation he had with a ten-year-old Octavia, who was worried she would never have breasts. He could still remember the look of horror on their foster mother's face when she walked in on him telling Octavia all the things he had learned from the boys in the bathroom. "That's probably not a very good example, brat."

"You were the one good thing before Pop and Mama that I had in my life. You were my world, still are. You took care of me when I was sick, made me laugh when I was sad and encouraged me all my life." With tears streaming down her face, Octavia looked up at him and said shakily, "Jocelyn will be lucky to have you as a father, Chris, I know I was." Chris pulled her into his arms and held her as they cried.

Walking into the restaurant, Chris held the door as Tay sauntered in. They made a striking couple, both stunning and dynamic. Their conversation at his office had left them both emotionally and physically drained, and in dire need of food. Tay forced him to take her out when all he wanted to do was stay home and lick his wounds. But no, she kept at him until he finally caved in just to get her to shut up.

Standing in line waiting for the maitre d' to seat them, Chris let his gaze wander over the diners, nodding at a few acquaintances. Following behind the waiter, he took Tay's arm as they wandered through the maze of tables heading towards their own. Tay stopped abruptly in the middle of the aisle, causing him to run into her back.

"Watch out," he said, laughing as he plodded into her from behind.

"Isn't that Eliza?" she asked, nodding to a table in the corner.

Turning quickly, Chris scanned the area she gestured to, freezing when he saw Eliza in the corner with another man. The man was leaning forward and lightly touching her face with the back of his hand.

"What the fuck?" he fumed. How the hell was she going to tell him she loved him and then go out to an intimate dinner with another man? Spinning, Chris turned to head over to her table, but Tay grabbed his arm and stopped him.

"What do you think you're doing?" she demanded in a hushed tone.

"I'm going over there..."

"And what, make a complete ass of yourself?" Pulling him to their table, she stood in front of him until he grudgingly sat down.

"I wasn't going to cause a scene," Chris denied, glaring at the couple.

"Yeah right," she snorted, sitting in her chair. "You were just going to go over there and ask them how the breadsticks are."

"I just want to know who he is."

"It's not your business, Chris."

"The hell it isn't."

"Are you going to look at the menu?"

"No..."

"Pick up the menu."

"But..."

"Pick up the menu before I bash you over the head with it."

"When did you get so damn bossy?" Frowning, he picked up the menu, but looked around it, trying to catch a glimpse of Eliza.

"Despite what you see in movies, brother dear, women don't like men who try to prove their love by making an ass of themselves in public."

"For the last time, I wasn't going to make a scene."

"Look, if its any consolation, they don't look like they're having a good time."

Craning his neck, he moved his head around and tried to see Eliza's expression. From this distance, he couldn't see anything, but he was hoping Tay was right. He knew he was the one that had suggested she go out with other people, but he didn't mean it. And more importantly, she should have known that.

"Would you stop it?" Octavia hissed, looking over her menu. "I didn't drive two hours over here to bail you out of jail. Don't make me call Mama, boy."

"Do you think they're out on a date?"

"I don't know, and furthermore, I don't care. Neither do you. Remember?"

"She does look upset, doesn't she? I wonder what's wrong." Worry clouded his eyes as he peered at his sister.

"Umm, let me think?" Rolling her eyes, she set her menu down. "Could it be that dufus she has the unfortunate luck to be in love with told her he doesn't love her, and she doesn't stand a chance with him?"

"I never said that I didn't love her." He scowled.

"Really? Did you say that you did?"

"Well no, but Eliza isn't one to cry. You don't know her."

"And neither do you, because from where I'm sitting if she's been crying, from the looks of that guy, she won't be crying alone for too long."

That was not what he wanted to hear. Eliza and her companion stood up, and headed towards the door. Where were they going? They had better not be going back to his place. Just the thought of that gigolo swooping down and hitting on her when she was obviously upset really pissed him off. Growling, he stood up, pausing when Tay grabbed his wrist.

"Where are you going?" she demanded.

"To cause a scene."

Walking across the restaurant, he bobbed and weaved his way through the crowd, calling Eliza's name as they reached the door. Eliza spun around, looking to see who had called her name.

"Eliza," he said, waving his arm above his head.

"Chris." Shocked, she turned to him and asked, "What are you doing here?"

Up close, Chris could tell something had been bothering her. Her face was slightly flushed, and her eyes were tinted red. If this jerk-off had done anything to her, he would have to answer to Chris.

"Eating dinner with Tay," he answered. "What are you doing here?"

"Can we help you?" her companion asked, coming up behind them, placing his arm around Eliza.

"Who are you?" Chris asked, turning towards him. He was barely able to contain his fury at the sight of this man touching Eliza.

"The question is, who are you?"

This guy's demeanor hinted at a familiarity Chris knew he had no right to feel, not with his woman anyway. Seeing red, Chris become furious when he saw the man squeeze her shoulder lovingly. "I'm the man who's going to rip your arm from your socket, if you don't take your hand off of her."

Gasping, Eliza reached up and gripped the man's hand, which only pissed Chris off even more. "It's okay, Anthony, this is Chris, my former boss."

"Former..." Chris's eyes narrowed in irritation. "Can I speak to you outside?"

"Don't you think you've done enough?" Anthony's tone lowered menacingly.

"What I think is..."

"Five minutes," Eliza said, nodding to Anthony.

Chris resisted the urge to gloat, but only barely. Following her out of the restaurant, Chris had to speed up his pace to keep up with her.

As soon as they cleared the doorway, Eliza turned to him angrily and demanded, "What do you want, Chris?"

"Who the hell is that guy?" he questioned, looking over his shoulder, at the man standing inside.

"Why do you care?" she asked annoyed. "I have never been so embarrassed in my entire life. How dare you act like that?"

"Are you on a date with him?"

"Do you even hear me?"

"Are you going home with him?"

"I've already been home with him," she yelled at a shocked Chris. "For over twenty years. He's my brother, Anthony."

Relief soared through his body, lifting his spirit and freeing his heart. "Oh."

"Oh! Is that all you have to say?" Eliza demanded, amazed. "You act like a big ass, and you say, *oh*. Chris, you're a dick."

Turning away, she moved to go back inside, but Chris grabbed her arm and turned her around. Tears spilled down her face, causing Chris to freeze. He would have never thought Eliza would cry. Not over him. Pulling away, she walked stiffly from him back towards the restaurant.

"Don't, Eliza." Walking towards her, he tried to touch her but she pulled away. "Don't do that, baby. Tell me what's wrong?"

"I'm not your baby. I'm not your anything."

Fresh tears streamed down her face, leaving him feeling mad and afraid. "That's not true."

"Sure, it is; I'm just your secretary."

"You're more than that. Eliza." Reaching for her again, he took her hand and pulled her to him. "Come home with me please, let's talk."

Biting her bottom lip, Chris could tell she was trying to decide what to do. "Just to talk, just to talk."

"Let me go tell Anthony."

"No," he said, stopping her. He was afraid if he let her go back in there she would change her mind. Reaching into his side pocket, he pulled out his cell and dialed his sister's number.

"Octavia Wilson".

"Hey, Tay, do me a favor."

"Where are you?"

"Eliza and I are going to my house to talk."

"And how am I supposed to get my car?"

"You know that guy she was sitting with?"

"The angry guy you almost came to blows with?" she questioned, irritated.

"Yes, that's her brother. Explain to him what's going on and ask him for a lift."

"Are you kidding?"

"I owe you one."

"Chris, this isn't funny."

"Thanks a million." Chris hung up as she bellowed his name again, and smiled at Eliza. "She said no problem," he lied with a straight face.

Taking Eliza's hand, he led her to the car, and shut the door. Looking up, he saw Tay and Anthony rush out of the restaurant's door. Lifting his hand, he waved before getting in his car and starting it up. They yelled his name as he backed up.

"Did you hear that?" Eliza asked, looking over her shoulder.

Reaching over, he patted her leg, drawing her attention back to him. "No," he said as he took off down the street.

Chapter Fifteen

Following Chris into his darkened house, Eliza was very apprehensive about being there. She was in absolutely no mood to fight with him. After the emotionally draining day she had had, all she had wanted to do was to have a nice dinner, a strong glass of wine and go to bed. But all that seemed like a distant dream now.

Chris turned on the light and gestured for her to have a seat. Removing his coat, he draped it on the arm of his couch and stood in front of her nervously.

"Do you want anything to drink?" he asked softly.

"No," she replied, sitting back on the couch. Kicking off her shoes, Eliza brought her feet up on the couch next to her, watching him as he paced back and forth. Chris was far from his usual polished self, which was refreshing to her, because for once, Eliza didn't feel like she was alone in her confusion.

"I feel like I need to apologize for the way I treated you tonight. Hell, for the way I've been treating you this whole time." Looking over at her, he seemed tense as if prepared to do battle. Battling was the last thing on her mind tonight.

"I didn't come here to fight with you, Chris."

"Good, because to tell you the truth, Eliza, I think I'm all fought out. I've been fighting since I was a kid, and I'm done." Chris stopped pacing and knelt in front of her. Placing his hands on her legs, he looked up at her imploringly. "I want to be with you, I know that, but I'm scared of what can happen."

Reaching out, Eliza caressed the side of his face lovingly. "Is the thought of being with me scarier than the thought of being without me?" she asked tenderly.

"No."

"This is where I get confused. I don't see the problem here, Chris." Pulling back, she sat back on the couch, confusion filling her eyes. "If you want to be with me, then be with me. This back and forth stuff is for the birds."

"I know, Eliza," he said, standing up and backing way. Walking towards the fireplace, he stared at the picture of Tay and said, "I'm afraid of what can happen. Of what I'm capable of."

"You're capable of love."

"If I hurt you, I won't be able to stand myself."

"Chris, I'm hurting now." Standing, she walked behind him and laid her hand on the back of his shirt. Eliza's heart was breaking in two, and this time not because he was hurting her, but because he was hurting himself.

"Tonight," he said, gripping the mantel tighter. "When I saw you with your brother, I wanted to smash his face in. Just the thought of you with another man had me on the verge of losing it. All my life I've been working hard on keeping my monster at bay, but when I'm around you, it feels like he's simmering on the top, trying to work his way out. I could hurt you, Eliza. I wanted to hurt Anthony tonight."

"But you didn't."

"But I could have, and that's the point."

"No, Chris." Turning him to face her, Eliza reached out and took his hand in hers. "The point is you didn't."

Looking up at him, Eliza asked, her voice full of love, "Do you know just how amazing you are? You grew up with the shittiest of the shitty childhoods and you came out on top. You have friends and family who love you, and there's a little girl I know who thinks you walk on water."

Laughing softly, he asked, "What did you and Tay do, start a 'we love Chris' fan club?"

"No, but I'd be the president if there was one. Chris, you are so much more than you realize, and maybe that's what makes you so great, the fact that you don't know it. But everyone else around you does. I know it. I've known it from the first day I started working for you."

Eliza fought back the tears burning in her eyes. Looking into his eyes, she poured all the love she felt for him into her next words. "I'm not afraid of you, and I trust you so much I'm willing to put the thing I love the most in your hands, my daughter. We can be a family. We can make new memories, good memories, but for every good memory we make, you have to toss out an old one until there's no old memories left to toss out."

Chris reached out to her and pulled her into him tightly. Laying his head on the top of hers, Eliza felt him inhale deeply as if trying to surround himself with her scent. Wrapping her arms around him, she held on to him and gave him the comfort he had been denied so often as a child.

Picking his head up, Chris pulled back and said to her gently, "I want everything you're saying, but it's going to take time for me to get there."

"I know."

"I...I care for you so much."

Smiling sadly, Eliza realized he was afraid she would leave if he didn't say the words. "I want to hear you say you love me, but only when you can, not forced or rushed."

"I just don't want to lose you," he admitted brokenly. "I need you too much."

"Well, I guess I could always postpone my resignation," she teased through her tears. Eliza had been waiting for this for a while. She knew Chris loved her. There was not a doubt in her mind. She didn't need to hear him say it right now, as long as he said it soon.

Snorting, he asked, laughter lightening his eyes, "What resignation?"

Pulling her into him again, Chris laid his head against hers and squeezed her tight. "Don't give up on me," he demanded.

"I won't, but you'll have to be the one to explain tonight to my brothers."

Laughing, he replied, "I'm willing to bet your brothers will understand a lot better than Tay."

"We'll see."

♦ ♥ ♣ ♠

"When you said I'd have to explain it to your brothers, I was thinking a one to one thing, not a huge family gathering." Chris looked around the driveway at the many cars parked and wondered to himself what the hell had he gotten himself into. When Eliza said she wanted him to go with her to dinner at her brother's, he thought maybe a small intimate dinner, not this.

"Are your parents here?" he asked as she bent over and unbuckled Jocelyn's belt.

"Of course they are."

"Well, how are they going to feel about you bringing me to dinner?"

Standing up she helped Jocelyn out of the car. Straightening her dress, she turned to him and smiled. "Is that what you worried about?"

"I'm not worried, merely curious. Are they going to freak out that you're dating a black man?"

"Well, they didn't when Anthony was, so I would assume not."

Chris's mouth dropped opened comically at her announcement. They had been spending a lot of time together the last couple of weeks, and they had talked about so many things regarding their families he was surprised to just now be hearing Anthony was gay.

Eyeing him over the roof of the metallic gray car, Eliza raised a brow and asked, "That's not a problem for you, is it?"

"No, just a surprise. You never mentioned it."

Shrugging her shoulders, she replied, "It never came up."

Walking around the car, he reached for her hand and the three of them walked to the door. Knocking, she stood up on her toes and kissed him quickly on the cheek. "Don't worry, *querido*, it's going to be fine."

"Who's worried?" he questioned, lying through his teeth. When Eliza had first mentioned him coming over, he wanted to refuse, but Chris knew being a part of a family meant actually having to be a part of the family. Eliza was really close to hers, so he needed to at least meet them.

A very pregnant woman opened the door, smiling brightly at them. "It's about time you guys got here. I need someone to save me from eating all the cake."

Walking in, Eliza embraced the woman, careful of her large stomach, and turned and introduced Chris.

"It's nice to meet you. I'm Veronica, and don't worry if you forget my name. You'll be meeting so many new people today," she said, giving him a quick hug. Bending over, she kissed Jocelyn on the head and stood back up, smiling. "Come in, come in."

They entered the house, and Chris looked around at the sinfully colorful house. This house would never be mistaken for a model home, but it had a warm inviting feel to it that his own home lacked. It might have something to do with the millions of pictures lining the shelves and walls, or the fact that the house was overrun with boisterous children and laughing adults who filled the home from corner to corner.

Jocelyn grabbed his hand and pulled him forward, introducing him proudly from one relative to the other. She chatted non-stop, but didn't let go of his hand so he could sneak away, not even for a second. More women embraced him today than in his entire life and he shook so many hands his arm began to stiffen. And the plates of food that kept coming at him reminded him of why he didn't go to his parents' house on Sundays.

Chris had wondered if they might be speaking Spanish or serving food there he was unfamiliar with, but that was hardly the case. The only thing missing from their barbeque was the collard greens his sister made like a pro. Everything else was the exact same. Of course, his father made better sauce, but it was still all good.

When Jocelyn began to fidget, he leaned down and told her it was okay for her to go and play. She ran off, but not before bringing her mother over to keep him company. She told him she didn't want him to be lonely. The thought of him being lonely in a house full of people amused him, but he could tell by her fierce expression she was serious. Eliza leaned against him and hugged his waist tightly. Leaning over, he placed his head on the top of her head and listened to the serenade of the voices in the background. If this is what family life was all about, it was something he could seriously get used to.

"Are you having a good time?" Eliza asked, rubbing his back soothingly through his shirt.

"I'm having a great time," he answered, and to his amazement, he really was. The only rough moment was when Anthony and her other two brothers approached him, but because Jocelyn refused to leave his side, he got only a mild warning. He'd have to make a mental note to buy the kid a fish after all, because he was sure she saved him from the dreaded speech he had tortured plenty of men with because of Tay.

Taking his hand, Eliza led him out of the house into the backyard. The sun was beginning to set and a soft breeze drifted across the yard. The party could still be heard from the garden, but it was less cluttered with family. A few people strolled about, smiling at them as they walked by. It seemed as if they weren't the only ones in the need for a little peace and quiet.

Peace and quiet was something he hadn't had a lot of lately, and for once he was very pleased about that. Before he couldn't wait to escape into the sanctuary of his house, away from everyone and everything, but lately he didn't want to be home unless Eliza and Jocelyn were there with him. It was actually nice to step over crayons and have a shelf of movies that didn't have any cursing. His house was finally beginning to feel more like a home now, and it was a feeling he wanted around him more and more.

"What do you think of my family?" Eliza asked as she leaned against him and watched the setting of the sun.

"In a word," he teased, "loud."

Laughing softly, Eliza pulled back and looked over her shoulder at him. "And what word would you use to describe your family?"

"Mom, Pops and Tay or you and Jocelyn?" he asked, looking down into her surprised face.

"We're family now, huh?" Tears misted her eyes at his comment.

"You got a problem with that?" he asked huskily.

"Not a one."

"Good." Leaning down, he placed a soft kiss on her lips. "Because I've been thinking."

"Yeah?"

"I still have one fantasy of yours to fulfill."

"That's right, isn't it?"

"Well I've been giving this a lot of thought, and I think I know you well enough that I could probably guess what your next fantasy is."

"Really?"

"The way I look at it is, you gave me your trust when you left me alone with Jocelyn. You gave me your heart when I wined and dined you. So the only thing left is..."

"Yes."

"Sex." Laughing, she pulled back and slapped him lightly on his chest. "No seriously, by the third date you're supposed to be putting out."

"What do you call the wall, the desk, the couch, the bed?"

"Appetizers." Bending, he kissed her lightly on her lips. Laughing, Eliza grabbed his hand and took him behind a tree. Pushing him back against the tree, she slid her hand under his shirt. Lightly scraping her nails down his chest, Eliza teased his nipples, dragging a sound of approval from his throat.

"Well, I've been thinking long and hard about it too," she said, smiling at his groan of arousal.

"Really?"

"Oh yeah," she teased.

"Does it involve sex?" he asked hopefully.

"Only if you play your cards right."

"Last time I played with you I won big," he said, wrapping his arms around her body. Chris pulled her in tight to him and rested his head against hers.

Eliza had kept her promise, he thought fondly. She and Jocelyn had begun to make new memories for him that were slowly but surely wiping away the painful ones from his past. Cradled in her arms, Chris now slept at night, no longer waking from dreams of the past, but now lulled by love, he rested, his soul at last at ease. He was finally breaking free of his childhood, and able to see into a future filled with children and laughter, filled with the love of Eliza.

"I was hoping you'd see it that way."

"I do," Chris said seriously. Pulling back, he looked into her tear filled eyes. "I love you, you know."

Smiling, Eliza said quietly and surely, "Of course I know. I've always known that."

Epilogue

Missy glanced up from her textbook and peeked over the counter, looking for signs of intelligent life forms in need of her help. Intelligent life forms in an adult bookstore, she thought with a giggle, like that was really going to happen. Not that she had anything against the late night visitors who gifted her with their presence. If it weren't for people shopping for porn and vibrators at ten o'clock at night, she wouldn't have a job. A job she needed and really liked, despite the location and the merchandise.

Glancing at her wristwatch, she mentally gave herself another ten minutes before she would go bang on the doors of the movie booths to rouse the late night whackers, so they would hurry up and she could close up. Not wanting to interrupt their jerks, she always coughed loudly before hitting the doors. No need to scare someone into accidentally spraying on the screen. Not that she was going to clean it up if they did. She didn't make that much money here.

The bell above the door dinged, alerting Missy of customers entering the store. Setting down her book, she pushed her glasses up on her small pug nose. When she glanced at the door, her plastic welcome smile turned into a sincere one as she saw her friend Kayla and another woman entering. Walking from behind the counter, she embraced the multicolored-dressed Kayla, who was beaming as usual. Kayla was one of the few people she knew who constantly had a smile on her face.

"Hi, what are you doing here so late?" Missy asked pulling back.

"We're here to buy an engagement present for Eliza," Kayla said pulling the other woman forward.

"You're buying her an engagement present here?"

"Hey, it's the gift that keeps on giving."

Laughing, Missy followed them to the vibrator aisle, still keeping a glance out at the counter. It wasn't that she was worried someone might want to make off with a vibrator, because her policy was, if anyone needed a vibrator so badly that they had to steal it, then they were welcome to it.

Holding up a large green vibrator, Eliza asked jokily, "Hmm, when you see this what comes to mind?"

"Ointment," Missy teased, causing them all to break out into laughter.

"Okay, what about this?" Holding up a large lava lamp shaped butt plug, Kayla asked.

"That you have to tweak your nipples to turn it on."

"My theory," Missy said, very dignified-like, "is if you can take something that large in your ass, do you really need it?"

The women burst out laughing at the assortment of gadgets surrounding them. Missy often thought the devices were silly, but it wasn't like she could ask a customer who was buying one, what the hell were they thinking.

The bell rang again, and she stepped out of the aisle and watched as several tuxedo-clad men entered the building.

"Hubba hubba ding ding, baby, you got everything," Kayla said, stepping into the aisle with her, eyeing the gorgeous men.

Elbowing her, Missy muttered, drooling herself "You're engaged, back off."

"Engaged, honey, not blind."

Smiling, Missy walked back to the counter and went behind the desk. Sitting on her stool, she shuffled her feet back and forth, eyeing the men as they strolled down the aisle. There was absolutely nothing sexier in the world than hot men dressed in tuxedos. Nothing.

"Missy," Kayla called from the toy section. "Eliza needs to know which anal plug you would recommend."

Red heat flushed her cheeks as several of the tuxedo-clad men turned in her direction. Ducking her head, she hid her scarlet face behind her chestnut brown hair and hopped off the stool. She was going to kill Kayla, she fumed silently to herself as she hurried from behind the counter. One of the reasons she liked being back there was because it hid her plump figure, which was exactly what she wanted to do when she was in the presence of mouth-watering men. Hide.

"Did you have to yell that?" she muttered to a laughing Kayla.

"Oops, my bad," Kayla teased. Picking up a plug, she said, "Eliza here is working up the nerve to have anal sex, much to the delight of Chris, I might add, and she's looking for a starter kit."

"A starter kit, huh?" Missy's whiskey brown eyes crinkled in delight. She could see why Kayla liked to tease so much.

"Chris is trying to weasel his way out of my third fantasy by insisting on this as his reward for fulfilling his end of the bet."

"What bet?" asked Missy.

"Better yet, what was the third fantasy?" Kayla asked.

"Forget I said anything," Eliza remarked, blushing.

"I don't think so," Kayla said, leaning against the dildo display. "Inquiring minds want to know."

"Okay, I'll tell if you tell about a certain phone call you made awhile back."

"Never mind," Kayla muttered looking down. Her cheeks begin to show a hint of pink, which only spurred Missy's curiosity further.

"Why do I feel left out?" she asked looking at the two women.

"Hey, do you play poker?" quipped Kayla. "Maybe you can come to one of our games."

"No, I don't..."

"Excuse me," said a deep masculine voice from behind. Turning around, Missy looked into the eyes of her former college English teacher, Professor Brody Kincaid. "I would like to be rung up."

"Sure, no problem," Missy said, scampering around him. Walking quickly to the front of the store, Missy reminded herself it was highly unlikely he would even recognize her. Out of a sea of students, she doubted she stood out. Not one to call attention to herself, she never raised her hand to answer questions and never showed up too early or too late for class. Missy had crafted the art of blending into a science.

Standing behind the counter, she studied him while he put his items on the counter. Dressed like the other men who had walked in, he was wearing a tuxedo without the tie, with the first few buttons undone. His black hair was full and thick and lightly touched the collar of his shirt. In a word, Missy thought, he was delicious.

Ringing up his purchases, she tried hard not to notice what he bought, but that was like trying not to stare at an accident. Missy really wanted to know though, what a man that attractive needed with a blow-up doll and handcuffs. It wasn't like the doll was going to go anywhere, but working here she had seen stranger things.

"So, Melissa Haddan, should I worry you're going to try to use this to change your grade on your transcripts?" he teased, as she picked up the pussy lollipops.

Glancing up startled, she looked into his large gray eyes. She was surprised he had even noticed her, let alone knew who she was. "Umm, of course not, sir," she stuttered as she shoved the pussies into the bag.

"I was joking," he assured her, causing her blush brighter. "I'm just surprised to see you here."

"I guess I could say the same."

Chuckling, he nodded his head in agreement. "Touché, Ms. Haddan. But see, I could always use the bachelor party as my excuse."

"Well, then I guess I'll just use the need to pay my bills." Missy wasn't used to men paying her this much attention. The way he was looking at her made her feel warm and itchy. Like her skin didn't fit. It was very unsettling, but oddly good at the same time.

Stepping back from the counter, he looked down the row of impulse items and selected a pair of racy playing cards. Tossing them on the counter, he reached in his jacket pocket and pulled out his wallet.

"Did I hear you correctly, that you don't know how to play poker?"

"Yes."

"That's a shame. I happen to be a poker aficionado."

"Really? It is a shame, you're right," agreed Missy, "because I've always wanted to learn how to play."

"It's not too late," he said, handing her the money.

"What do you mean?"

"I'd be more than willing to teach you."

"Oh, I don't know," Missy hesitated. "That's probably not a good idea."

"Anthony Holden said, 'Whether he likes it or not, a man's character is stripped bare at the poker table; if the other players read him better than he does, he has only himself to blame. Unless he is both able and prepared to see himself as others do, flaws and all, he will be a loser in cards, as in life.' And I would have to say I wholeheartedly agree. There's a science to it, an art if you dare, but truly when it comes down to it, it's all about how well you know yourself, and how far you're willing to go."

Missy felt the urge to look behind her, to make sure the looks of interest she thought he was sending her were really for her. Reaching into the register, Missy took out his change, praying it was the right amount. Feeling flustered, she thrust the money at him. Reaching for the change, Brody lightly brushed his fingers against hers as he took the money. Her pulse flickered beneath her skin, joining the erratic beating of her heart.

Brody's gaze flickered to her lips when she licked at them nervously, before swinging back to her eyes. Reaching into his wallet, he pulled out a business card and slid it across the counter towards her. Picking up his bag, he asked her, "How far are you willing to go, Melissa?"

About the Author

Lena Matthews spends her days dreaming about handsome heroes and her nights with her own personal hero. Married to her college sweetheart, she is the proud mother of an extremely smart toddler, three evil dogs, and a mess of ants that she can't seem to get rid of.

When not writing, she can be found reading, watching movies, lifting up the cushions on the couch to look for batteries for the remote control and plotting different ways to bring Buffy back on the air.

You can contact Lena through her website: www.lenamatthews.com.

Look for these titles

Now Available

Something Old, Something New
Joker's Wild: Call Me

Coming Soon:

Joker's Wild: Stripped Bare

GREAT
cheap
FUN

Discover eBooks!

THE FASTEST WAY TO GET THE HOTTEST NAMES

Get your favorite authors on your favorite reader, long before they're
out in print! Ebooks from Samhain go wherever you go, and work with
whatever you carry—Palm, PDF, Mobi, and more.

samhain
publishing, Ltd

WWW.SAMHAINPUBLISHING.COM

LaVergne, TN USA
10 November 2009
163620LV00002B/15/A